On the
Wings of Love

Veronika Sophia Robinson

Sweet Cinnamon
Romance

For every person
with an inner minx.

Veronika Robinson is an Australian author living in rural Cumbria, England, with her husband, Paul, and two black cats, Kali and Pelé, in a three-hundred-year-old cottage overlooking the Pennines. As a teenager, she devoured romance novels instead of biology textbooks, and was regularly given detention by her science teacher for drawing "the wrong sort of hearts"!

In her mid twenties, after kissing too many frogs, Veronika met her soul's love, Paul. It was at this time that she became a marriage celebrant. All these years later, she still writes and officiates beautiful wedding ceremonies. Although voted by her secondary-school teachers as the student most likely to fail in life, Veronika couldn't be happier with the way she spends her days.

A late bloomer, in her mid-fifties she earned her Master's Degree in Creative Writing from the University of Cumbria, despite no previous academic qualification. A prolific writer, her books span fiction and non-fiction.

On The Wings Of Love
© Veronika Sophia Robinson
© Cover illustration by Heidi Harbers
Published by Sweet Cinnamon Romance
An imprint of Starflower Press
ISBN: 978-1-7398336-8-8
St. Valentine's Day 2023

A CIP catalogue record for this book is available from the British Library.

Published by Sweet Cinnamon Romance, an imprint of Starflower Press www.starflowerpress.com

Books by the same author at www.veronikarobinson.com

A Sweet Cinnamon Romance
will surprise you!

Green With Envy

'What the hell?!' Ashley Lyndhurst yelled as he took in the sight before him. Nothing he'd ever experienced in his life, personally or professionally, could have prepared him for this moment. This was *not* how he left his palatial penthouse suite two weeks ago.

Not for a second did he dare step inside. Every square inch of the pure-wool merino carpet was now... What was it? Ashley moved closer, then bent down just in case his eyes were deceiving him. No. Surely not? How was that even...*possible*?

Alfalfa sprouts, about five centimetres high, had their fibrous roots firmly embedded into the carpet. Wall-to-wall green, that's all he saw: little leaves waving up at him as if to say 'Have a great day!'

The carpet would have to be stripped. Replaced. With his heart pounding against his ribcage, he wondered if all the rooms were like this. Careful step by careful step, he walked across the room, leaves scrunching beneath his Italian hand-made shoes, then opened the door to his bedroom. No. *No!*

More green carpet, and worse: every item of clothing in his wardrobe had been removed and cut to ribbons: all left in a pile on his king-sized bed. A fabric mountain of tailor-made suits discarded like scrap material in a clothing factory. For a man who commanded international boardrooms and was frequently invited to speak at prestigious conferences, Ashley Lyndhurst was speechless. Who'd do this to him? Ashley had no enemies, at least not of the revengeful, destructive sort. This was clearly the work of... a woman. A *jilted* woman. But, try as he might, he simply couldn't imagine anyone from recent years who'd go to such lengths to make a point. As he stepped back on the simultaneously crunchy and soggy carpet, he once again surveyed the living room floor.

What on Earth was that in the corner of the hallway? Three hundred silk ties all dipped in... 'What is that?' he said out loud. *A basin of blood?* Upon further inspection he realised it was nothing more than food colouring. Who would do this? Jade would be livid. The vast majority of the ties were ones she'd specifically chosen for him from various airport locations around the world.

Ashley's thoughts hurtled through time and space. He'd only come home for an overnighter before heading away on his next business trip. Time was of the essence. Right now, he had to get someone to sort this mess out. Pronto! Where was Jade when he needed her? If anyone could handle it, she could. Ashley hoped she was over her cold. This past fortnight without her had been unbearable. Jade was his right hand girl, and his right hand just hadn't been the same.

Ashley headed for the central-heating switch. The place was stifling. Why would the heating be on in the middle of Summer? For a few moments, he looked helplessly at his bespoke designer shoes. To help alfalfa seeds grow, that's why the heating was on! Thousands of them. Thousands of tiny seeds. It started to fall into place. Yes, sprinkle millions of alfalfa seeds into a bed of beautiful, natural-fibred carpet, turn on the fire sprinklers and give them a handsome soaking, then put them to bed with 25 Celsius-degree heat, and leave them to grow. Damn it. Damn whoever did this!

Jade. He had to get Jade to sort this mess out. And one by one, his thoughts rolled on, not wanting to make the connection.

Jade Stirling?

That could be the only explanation. No. Ashley didn't want to entertain the possibility. Not Jade.

She was the only person in the world who had access to this place. But *why*? Surely he'd been a good employer? Six weeks annual holiday; personal pension; countless other perks. Why would she do this?

Ashley recalled their last conversation, then changed his mind. No, it couldn't be Jade. Sure, she might have had access, but she didn't have *cause*. Nothing about this made any sense.

Jade was a kind person; thoughtful, friendly, compassionate, and without a nasty bone in her body. It was true that she liked a good laugh, and was a practical joker, but this wasn't funny. And then Ashley thought of that laugh, and what a hole Jade's absence had left during his recent business trip.

Ashley couldn't stay in the room. Everything had to be stripped. But first, he had to find Jade.

He dialled the office on his mobile.

'Lyndhurst Incorporated, Hannah speaking. How may I help you?' The person's voice was soft and sweet, but it was not Jade. Where was Jade? Reliable Jade? Always-there-at-every-turn Jade?

'Where's Jade?' His voice was brusque.

'Jade doesn't work here any more. May I take a message, sir? I am sure Human Resources could pass it on to her. Is it personal or professional?'

'My name is Ashley Lyndhurst. Hannah, I'm your employer. Where the hell is Jade?'

'Mr Lyndhurst. I'm so sorry,' she fumbled over her words. 'Jade refused to give us any forwarding details. She said…' Hannah was clearly distressed and couldn't continue.

7

'Never mind. I'll be there in twenty minutes. You can tell me then.' Without a word of goodbye or thank you, he ended the call.

What the hell was Jade playing at? For more than seven years she'd worked for him, both day and night. Ashley trusted her with his life. And then it hit him, right there where it hurt: *Jade was his whole world.* Damn it, she even picked out his ties for him! His ties. His 300 now permanently blood-red ties!

Once again, he searched his memory banks; this time furiously looking for a shred of reason for Jade's uncharacteristic outburst.

Jumping into the limo, he instructed the driver to take him straight back to the office.

'No Jade with you today, sir?' the elderly man asked politely. 'Is she still unwell?'

Even the driver expected them to be together! They were always together! She was his *everything*. Jade filled his diary. Jade shielded him from prowling women of a certain age. Jade bought his clothes. Jade brought him coffee. Jade made him laugh. And that was what was wholly missing from this day: *Jade*. But what the hell was his penthouse alfalfa jungle all about? It couldn't be Jade! It was incongruous.

Had he been unkind? Did he not express his appreciation for her? Ashley may have lost his temper with other staff members, but *never* with Jade. There was never a single occasion in which he had been cross or terse with her. Her work was impeccable.

'No, no Jade today, I'm afraid.' Ashley buried his head in some paperwork as they weaved their way across the city, through traffic lights and honking horns and London fumes. Ashley couldn't concentrate; he was used to her being at his side. Jade was the voice of reason; the sound of laughter to lighten tense negotiation days; a warm smile to melt him when business became overwhelming; the listening ear of someone who cared.

She cared? Of course she cared. But, did she care too much?

Or was the truth that Ashley Lyndhurst cared too much for her? Maybe he shouldn't have given her time off for what was nothing more than the common cold.

Three months ago she'd asked for a reference. There was a wonderful job in Boston that would be perfect for her. Ashley recalled writing the reference. It was one of distinction. Of course he'd make sure that she'd get the job, if that's what she really wanted. But it wasn't what *he* wanted. No, not at all. Even then, he knew he'd be lost without her. Everyone knew that Jade was the best PA in all of Europe, and probably the finest in the aviation industry.

'Sir? We're here, sir.' The driver prompted him. So far away from the present moment, Ashley didn't notice they were in front of the London offices for Lyndhurst Incorporated: worldwide chartered flights for VIPs.

'Thanks Max. You can have the rest of the day off. Pick me up at six.'

The specially designed building was an elliptical glass tower with a circular perimeter, and lent an imposing presence to the central business district.

Ashley's thoughts returned to Jade's job application. It was successful, of course, and she'd been offered the role without an interview. One look at a reference from Lyndhurst Incorporated and the job was hers. At the time, Ashley had turned up at her London apartment and offered to double her salary immediately. Annual leave was doubled. Then he expanded her already ridiculously large wardrobe allowance, and offered to buy the apartment for her. There wasn't anything he wouldn't do to keep his cherished employee. Ashley knew she was a one-of-a kind, and truly irreplaceable.

'Let me think about it,' was all she said that night.

At seven the next morning, she was at his penthouse packing his suitcase for their next overseas meeting. And life continued as if she'd never even applied for the job. Not another word was mentioned. It never occurred to him that she wasn't happy. 'Alfalfa sprouts, Jade? What were you thinking?'

'Hannah, is it?' he asked the young girl in his office.

She mumbled.

Ashley shook his head. This girl would never do. What was Jade trying to prove?

'Did Jade employ you?' he asked soberly.

'Yes, sir. Jade said I was everything you needed.'

'Did she now?' He couldn't help smile. Jade gave him the exact opposite of what he needed: a timid, mumbling, personality-free PA. She'd pay for this! But first, he had to find her.

'Did she give you any indication of where she was going to? Any hint at all?' He searched Hannah's eyes for a clue.

'No sir. I overheard her talking to the accountant. She told Fred to stop all payments, including pension, allowances and holiday money. She said all her bank accounts were closed, and that she was severing all ties with Lyndhurst. Well, actually, what she said was: all ties with *Ashley* Lyndhurst...'

'Okay, I get the picture. Hannah, you can work

out on front reception with Emilia. I'm fine to deal with my own business for the day. Thank you.'

Hannah stumbled over her feet, grabbing his desk for support, before pushing her thick, black-framed glasses back over her freckled nose. 'I'm sorry, sir.' Her garbled words fought to compete with the groan of her shock as she tripped unceremoniously over her platform heels.

'Just perfect, Jade. Just perfect,' he muttered under his breath. 'So, you think you've had the last laugh. We'll see about that. I'll find you!'

One thing he knew, though, was that through her seven years of working with him, Jade was well connected. If she contacted any of his colleagues in the industry, they'd give her a job without a reference. Everyone knew that Ashley Lyndhurst was part of a team. A two-person team: Ashley and Jade. Colleagues never believed Ashley when he said his relationship with Jade was strictly platonic. 'She's my PA,' he insisted over and over.

What work would she look for? Ashley knew she was capable of being so much more than a PA, but he'd held her back. Yes, that was the ugly truth: Ashley Lyndhurst prevented her from reaching her full potential. Why? So he could reach his. Each time she wanted to stretch her wings, literally, he held her back. It was unthinkable that she'd work anywhere else. Uncomfortably, he recalled the panic he felt when she received her commercial pilot's licence, and she hinted that it wouldn't be long now. Jade said she could fly anywhere in the world. Well, yes she could, but she wouldn't. Ashley wouldn't allow that. The irony was that he'd paid for the vast majority of her flying lessons and exams; given her wings, and then clipped them.

A sharp knock jolted Ashley from his thoughts.

'Come in!'

'Ash,' came the purr of a feline-looking woman from the doorway. 'Ash, how are you?'

Leonie Allan stood there, six foot tall, long blonde hair, and Barbie-doll body. She worked in Human Resources, and he'd taken her on his last overseas trip. Jade had been feeling a bit under the weather, and he insisted she stay home. Leonie accompanied him. It had been an administrative disaster. Turned out she could barely type, and spent more time painting her fingernails than taking down his dictation.

'Leonie, come in. What can I do for you?' The words had no sooner left his mouth, as he took in her long, lithe frame, than the strangest notion occurred to him. *Was Jade jealous?* Of Leonie? Impossible. *Leonie?* No way! There was nothing even remotely interesting about her. And even if he did fancy her, why would that concern Jade? Did...did she like him in that way?

Jade was just eighteen years old when she began working for him. Beautiful, vibrant, and passionate to be the best PA on the planet, she lived to be an employee he could be proud of. But she was little more than a girl out of school. Ashley couldn't look at her that way, and besides, it would have gone against company rules to have had a relationship. But that was then. The Jade of today was most definitely a woman. Ashley's mind wandered from Jade to Leonie, and back again. There was no comparison.

'So, your little Jade's gone?' she smirked. 'Who'd have thought that pretty little guard dog would ever leave your side? That girl was like a magnet. No, more like superglue! It's good for you that she's gone.'

'How the hell would you know what's good for

me?' He stood up, furiously realigning some paperwork on his desk.

'Come on Ash, it's common knowledge that she lived and breathed for you. What woman could compete with that? No woman wants to date a man whose PA turns up at seven every morning to help him dress.'

'How do you know that?' Ashley was indignant. 'Leonie, what do you want? Is there something I can help you with, or are you just here to gloat?'

'All I'm saying, Ash, is look for the silver lining. Now you can start to seriously date women instead of having to meet them in a hotel rather than your own home. Everyone knows that you'd never take a woman home; not when Jade is capable of turning up at any time.'

'The gossip mill in this place is astounding.' With his back to her, Ashley pretended to search for something in his filing cabinet.

'By the way, here's your penthouse key. Jade's last words were something about watering your plants.' Leonie swung out of the door on her five-inch heels.

Ashley laughed out loud. Finally, he could see the funny side. Oh yes, she watered his plants alright. It was the standing joke around the office that Jade started every week watering all the office plants. No one got coffee or copies of memos until they were done, all seventy of the potted palms, philodendrons, lilies and spider plants that she'd adopted over the years to make the office "more friendly". Not even Ashley Lyndhurst was allowed to argue with that! Was she in love with him? Is that what this was all about? Was she furious with him for taking Leonie to New York? He had to find her!

Ashley walked to the main reception area. 'Emilia.

13

Hannah. Hold all my calls, unless it's Jade.'

They looked at each other.

'What?' he asked. 'Why are you looking at each other?'

Hannah froze. Emilia, more self-assertive, replied 'think of the words: Hell. Cold day. Freezes over. And then, think of them coming from Jade's pretty little mouth. Mr Lyndhurst, with all due respect, Jade is *not* going to phone you. Not today. Not any day.'

'Would someone tell me what the hell I've done?'

'Who,' came a mousy little voice from Hannah's direction.

'Sorry?' He leaned over his newest employee.

'The question should be "who" you've done,' she gulped, and then scurried away to do some filing.

'Who I've done? I haven't *done* anyone!'

'Jade thought differently. There's no need to explain it to us, sir. What you do away from this office isn't our business.'

'*Who* am I supposed to have done?'

'Oh, I don't know....take a wild guess. Malibu-blonde, legs like a giraffe, smells like a perfume factory, purrs like a cat on heat.'

'Enough, Emilia. I get the message. Jade thinks I've slept with Leonie? Seriously? Doesn't anyone around here know me?'

'I best get back to work, sir,' Emilia said, raising her eyebrows.

'Why would I sleep with her? Emilia?'

'A place like this thrives on rumours. You've got fifty staff members. People talk. Mr Lyndhurst, please don't take this the wrong way, especially coming from me, but you're an incredibly attractive man. You're also wealthy and powerful. Every woman wants to be noticed by you, and well, perhaps it takes a woman like Leonie, who, frankly, has no shame, to get your attention. Clearly Jade had no chance.'

'Jade had no chance for what?'

'Mr Lyndhurst, do I have to spell it out for you?'

'Spell what out!'

'Jade's in love with you; she has been for years. You broke her heart when you took Leonie away.'

'But it was business!'

'How was she to know that? Remember, Jade books all the accommodation when you're away. Maybe the idea of adjoining suites with a shared internal door, and Jacuzzi…'

Ashley rubbed his hand through his hair. He didn't need this. A lovesick ex-employee who took pleasure in destroying his penthouse.

'Where is she, Emilia? You must know.'

'My life is worth more than my job, sir. Jade and I are friends. My loyalty to her comes first,' she said, then turned her back on him.

'Has she threatened you? Emilia? Why can't you tell me? I need to talk to her. To explain…'

'I don't think that's a good idea, sir. Let her go. It's best this way.'

'Let me decide what's best. Please.'

'Jade was one of the best things about working here. She made everyone feel good about themselves. I value my friendship with her, and…look, Mr Lyndhurst. I'm not going to tell you, but it's not that hard to work out. Jade's more than a PA. You know that. She's got a pilot's license, and she knows as much about this industry as you. What would she do with her skills? Work it out. And just think outside the box. Think outside London. If she was, for example, and I'm not saying this is the case, I'm just throwing it out there,' she said, waving her hands around, 'if she was going to fly chartered flights for the rich and famous, where might she go? Whom might she work for? Assuming, of course, she didn't set up in direct competition with you.'

'She wouldn't! Would she?'

Ashley strode into his office. Unrequited love? This was all because he hadn't noticed her? As he sat back into his leather office chair, Ashley tapped his pen against the table. Jade Stirling. What was he going to do with her? How the hell was he going to find her?

For the next few hours, he scoured his contact list until he finally realised where she was. It was the obvious choice for a rookie pilot.

'Put me through to Tom Bradley, please. It's Ashley Lyndhurst in London.'

'Ash, mate. How are you?' came the broad Australian drawl down the line. 'How can I help you?'

'Jade. Is she with you?'

'All mine!' he laughed. 'I can't believe you let her go.'

'I didn't. She's broken her contract.'

'Mate, that's not how she tells the story. Look, I don't want a rift between you and I, but she's the best thing that could have happened to Roo Airlines. People fall in love with Jade. She's just got that something special, you know?'

'Is she your PA or a pilot?' Ashley had to know. Would she have given up her overpaid job to be someone else's PA?

'PA? No way. She's flying celebrities out to the interior. Places like Ayres Rock. Even though she's only been here five days, already we're getting in brilliant feedback. I'm afraid your loss is my gain.'

'Tom, I'm flying out there. Now. She has a contract with me.'

'Ashley. Let it be. Jade's happy here. In fact, one of our guys has even taken a shine to her. A man like you can surely get another PA. You can buy anyone in the world. Jade could do with a change.'

'I'll be there in less than forty eight hours, Tom. Make sure she's around.' Ash hung up the phone. Clothes. He had no clothes! The vision of them cut to ribbons on his bed haunted him. Jade knew he'd have to go shopping before he could come after her!

As his mind raced through the various women who worked in the building, he wondered if any of them was capable of restocking his wardrobe at such short notice? Jade. Jade could do it. But Jade was on the other side of the world. Flying planes! Damn it.

Jade was going to be the most expensive PA in existence, but he had to have her back. Ashley headed down to the ground floor, and caught a taxi to his favourite clothing shop. Several suits later, it occurred to him that the climate in Australia called for some more relaxed attire. It was only now that he appreciated all the work Jade had put in, usually after hours and in between flying lessons and studies, to replenish suits, ties, shoes, aftershave. That was it: she needed another pay rise. Why hadn't she just asked? Ashley renegotiated the contract in his head. Jade could have anything she wanted. All she had to do was name her price and he'd have her back as his PA in no time at all.

Down Under

Touchdown in Sydney, Australia, was gentle. Ashley Lyndhurst prided himself on such competent pilots. That's why his company had such a first-class reputation. There was nothing shoddy about their style, performance or level of service. A multi-million pound company rested on firm ideals, and reliable staff. Lyndhurst Incorporated had both.

Ashley wondered if everyone in his London office knew of Jade's spot of penthouse gardening. Now that he was on the other side of the world, he couldn't help but laugh. It was rather funny. Perhaps he'd nickname the place Jade's Garden. The strangest sensation kicked him in the guts. What was that? Yes, he missed her, but it wasn't about the way she expertly navigated his appointments and aligned his professional diary with his personal life so he could still see his mother and sisters. And it wasn't how she made his coffee to perfection. Nor was it the way she started each day with that perfect smile. There was something else. Something he couldn't quite put his finger on. Then he recalled the last time he saw her. Jade had turned up at his penthouse, with her travel bags; and her pert, upturned nose was red raw, and her eyes were streaming. Jade could hardly stand. 'It's just a cold,' she protested. 'I'll be fine after a good night's sleep.'

'You've been working long hours. It's my fault. I've been too demanding lately. You need some time off. Go home. I'll call you a cab. Don't worry about the trip. I'll manage. The only thing I want you to think about is getting better.'

Despite his kindness, she pleaded with him to let her go. Jade insisted that there wasn't anyone in the office who had a handle on the project. And, she said, she'd spent months preparing this contract for him. There was no way she wasn't going to be there for the signing. Jade stood in his penthouse, nearly passing out with exhaustion and refused to go. Ashley ended up sharing a taxi back to her apartment, and literally tucked her up in bed.

Ashley remembered looking at her: weak, tired, vulnerable. With his eye on the clock, and counting down the hours till the scheduled flight, he brought her a hot-lemon drink, topped up a hot-water bottle, and bid her farewell. Then he arranged with Emilia to come by each day and check up on Jade.

Leonie was beside herself with excitement when Ashley seconded her to be his temporary PA. Jade would have hated it, he knew that, but he had little choice as no one else was readily available.

Jade lived for her job, and Ashley Lyndhurst realised he had a lot of making up to do.

'Where is she, Tom?' he asked when walking into the air-conditioned offices of Roo Airlines. 'Where's Jade?'

'Just on her way back from the Great Barrier Reef. Take a seat, Ash. Marlene, would you bring Mr Lyndhurst and I some coffee, thanks?'

'Tom, she's coming back with me.'

'Mate, I don't know what went down with you two. Seriously, everyone in the business knows you two are inseparable. Whatever's happened—and she refuses to talk about it, so, frankly, I have no idea—one thing is clear: *she's mad as hell*. That's not a woman you want to approach without full-body armour. But, mad or not, she's a professional; and she's doing a great job. If you want her back, then you're on your own, mate.

You'll have to fight for her. I won't get in the way of that, you have my word. But I'm not going to make it easy, either. I'll throw incentives her way.'

'I appreciate that, Tom.'

Marlene served coffee, and once she was out of ear shot Ashley asked 'Where is she living?'

'Mate, I can't give you that information. You know I can't.'

'Tom, it's not as if I'm a stalker.'

'Tell me this, Ash. Why did you never marry Jade? Everyone but you seems to know you're meant for each other.'

'Marry? Because she's a girl!'

Tom laughed out loud. 'A girl? She was once, sure, but in case you haven't noticed she's somewhat of a woman now.'

'Yes, but...'

'Ash. Open your eyes.'

Ashley didn't want to think of her that way. It was too confusing. If he thought of her as a woman, he'd never be able to focus on the job at hand.

'Where is she living?' he asked again, this time more firmly.

Tom walked to a filing cabinet and opened a drawer. 'Don't do anything stupid,' he said, passing him some keys. 'She's staying in my holiday house in the Blue Mountains until she gets a place of her own.'

Tom scribbled down the address.

'Don't spook her! She's in contract to *me* now. Remember that.'

'I'll behave,' Ashley said, then gulped down his coffee. 'When is she due back?'

'Three hours from now. She'll check in, and then have three days off before her next chartered flight.

20

She's still pretty jet lagged from the London flight. Be nice to her!'

'See you later,' he said, then drove an hour and a half to the address Tom gave him.

The setting Sun blushed against the blue haze of the mountains, lighting up the rocks. Eucalyptus-scented air awakened his senses. Counting down the minutes until she returned, he wondered about how she'd feel seeing him sitting inside her temporary accommodation.

Tom's words caught him somewhere in the pit of his belly: *why did you never marry Jade?* Marry Jade? But he and Jade were...What were they? Boss and employee? Friends? Constant companions?

The sky-blue bungalow with a sweeping red corrugated-iron roof was low set, and surrounded by yellow wattle and crimson bottlebrush shrubs. It was away from other houses, down a dirt road, and enjoyed a private aspect facing the Sun.

Ashley unlocked the front door and let himself inside. Immediately, he was taken aback with the scent of Jade. Jade Stirling was living in someone else's house and yet it already smelt like her: jasmine and vanilla. Ashley sighed and missed her far more than he'd realised. Taunted by the aroma, he walked around the house looking for other signs of her. Although she'd kept it fairly tidy, she'd strewn some clothes across the sofa, and left half a dozen magazines underneath a dirty coffee cup. It made him laugh to think of her being so relaxed. No one in his office was allowed even a sip of coffee unless they were in arm's reach of a drinks coaster. As much as everyone loved Jade, she was known affectionately as the Coaster Police.

Ashley wandered into the bedroom. The scent followed him in there, and also leapt out at him. It was all he could do to catch his breath. This signature scent was the foundation of his life. Always there, within easy reach. Was that why he'd been so on edge for the past fortnight? Leonie's perfumes were highly irritating compared to the gentle essential oils Jade dabbed on her pulse points. At first, Ashley sat on the edge of her bed, and then he lay down. A handful of light paperbacks sat on the bedside table. What was she reading? Romance novels? SKY magazine for pilots? Ashley laughed out loud, and picked up one of the novels from the top of the pile. As he opened it, a piece of paper fell out. It was a brochure of Lyndhurst Incorporated, and it was folded over to reveal a photo of Ashley and Jade standing next to one of his planes.

Ashley had seen the photo a thousand times or more. There was a life-sized version in the main reception area of the London office. If she was so angry with him, why was this photo in here? Suddenly, he heard the sound of keys jangling at the front door. No. Not yet! He wasn't ready for her. Jade was early. Damn. In a moment of panic, he fell to the floor and rolled under her bed.

When she walked into the bedroom, Jade flicked on the bedside radio, and threw her pilot's bag onto the bed. Slow jazz tunes filled the room, and Ashley wondered how he'd explain himself if she looked under the bed. For now, he was safe. Within seconds, she'd stepped into the ensuite and turned on the shower. When the door closed behind her, Ashley rolled out from under the bed and stood up. And then, in a moment of Jade-inspired genius, Ashley opened the wardrobe and pulled out all of her clothes and threw them into the suitcase, and carried it out to the kitchen. Then he grabbed the other clothes which had lain across the sofa, and packed them away too. After hiding the suitcase in the far end of the pantry, he felt pretty pleased with himself. Jade would soon see what it was like to come home to no clothing. Ashley made himself a coffee, and then sat on the fabric-covered sofa. It wouldn't be long now. Even though jazz music played softly in the background, he could hear when the shower was turned off. The door opened, and a few moments later she opened the wardrobe door.

Silence. Nothing but the sweet sound of silence.

'What the hell?' she yelled, slamming the wardrobe door shut. Funny, they were the exact words Ashley had uttered when he came home to his miniature jade forest.

'Where the hell are my clothes?'

Ashley listened, with a smile on his face, as he heard her open drawers, and then curse. Finally she stomped her way into the lounge room, wearing nothing but a hot-pink towel around her body, and one, turban-style, around her head.

'Hello,' Ashley said, smiling. 'Missing something?' he laughed. The look on her face was priceless.

'You?' she gulped. 'You've taken my clothes?'

'I guess that makes us even,' and even after giving her his award-winning smile, she stood there, her face utterly confused.

'What are you doing here?' she demanded.

'Jade, I could ask you the same question. In fact, I will: Jade, what are you doing here?'

'That's none of your business. I'm free to change jobs if I want. You can't just go through life buying people, Ashley. I'm not for sale!'

23

'Well, you've made that abundantly clear,' he said, getting off the sofa and walking close to her.

'What are you doing?' she asked, when he was just centimetres away from her. 'What...'

But any intention of her interrogating him vanished beneath his lips. As Ashley's mouth found hers, slowly searching for a place of mutual satisfaction, he heard her moan gently.

'Is that what you wanted from me, Jade?' he asked, when they both came up for air. 'Didn't I pay you enough attention?'

'What...what are you talking about?'

Ashley watched her face go crimson, and a rash form upon her neck, then pulled her closer, breathing her in. No longer was she the young girl he employed, and no longer was she in his employ. Finally, he saw her as she was: a beautiful, desirable woman. Their tongues met in a tango. Seeking, hiding, searching, surrendering. The pleasure coursing through his veins astounded him. This hadn't been his intention. Kissing her was the last thing that had been on his mind, but when she walked out with just a towel around her, he saw her. For the first time, he truly saw her as a woman.

There was no way she'd come back to work now. He'd just violated his own code of conduct. It was unforgiveable.

'Ashley, stop,' she said.

'So, you don't want this?' he asked, confused. 'You don't want me to kiss you?'

'Did I ever say that I did? Have I ever said I wanted anything from you?'

'I don't understand. What do you want?'

As she pulled away, the loose tuck of her towel undid; and it fell straight to the floor, leaving them both catching their breath. Ashley didn't attempt to look away.

'Let me get it for you,' he offered, bending down to pick up the towel but never losing eye contact with her. Before wrapping it back around her, Ashley took her in: five feet and eight inches of unmistakeable beauty. The towel was secured firmly, but then he did something which took both of them by surprise: he reached for the towel on her head, and undid the turban, tossing it on the floor. Then, ever so slowly, his fingers tousled through her wet chocolate-brown hair, and he helped it to fall down around her shoulders.

'I never meant to hurt you,' he whispered. 'I was trying to protect you. You had a cold. You were in no state to travel. You know as well as I do how flying is not good when you've got a cold. I'm sorry, Jade.'

'I don't know what you're talking about,' she said, trying to remove his hands from her hair.

'I'm not going anywhere till we get this sorted, Jade.'

Once again, Ashley leaned in and kissed Jade. As he did so, he wondered if she'd imagined him holding her in this way for the last seven years. Is that why she'd tried different hairstyles, and changed fashions? Had she been trying to catch his attention? Is that why she was so perfect at her job?

'Mr Lyndhurst,' she said, adopting a formal tone, 'I don't know what possessed you to travel to the other side of the world to sort this out, but I no longer work for you. I am employed by Tom Bradley, and I suggest you leave.'

'No, Jade. Damn it. You can't just destroy a man's home, tear his clothing to shreds, dunk every tie he owns in red food colouring...'

'Ink. It's ink. It won't come out, I can promise you that!' When she tried moving away, he firmly brought her back in front of him.

'Ink, then.' Ashley was losing his patience. 'Why? What did I do?'

'If you have to even ask, then you don't deserve…'

'Deserve *what*, Jade?' At first, he turned away exasperated, and then faced her again. 'Do you love me, Jade? Is that what all of this is about?'

'Don't be ridiculous.' Like a rabbit in headlights, her face defied the words coming out of her mouth.

'Jade, if you want to leave this house at any time with clothes on, then you're going to have get real honest here…'

'You can't do that!'

'Watch me!' Ashley made himself comfortable on the sofa, and then smiled. 'Wouldn't mind another coffee. No one makes it quite like you.'

Jade screamed in exasperation. 'You're not meant to be here. You're not part of my plan!'

'And what plan would that be, Ms Stirling? What plan is that?'

'Ashley, I need you to leave. I know you're used to getting everything you want. One click of your fingers and people run like ants on a disrupted anthill to meet your every whim. I'm no longer one of those people. I don't work for you. You can't buy me. You don't own me.'

'But I believe you owe *me*, young lady. Let's see, four weeks of wages, thousands and thousands of pounds of new clothing, and then there's the little matter of carpet. So yes, Jade Stirling, you have a debt to pay. And I'm not leaving until it's settled. No, I'm not leaving at all.'

'You can't be serious? How the hell am I supposed to cover all those costs?'

'What, you mean Miss Perfectly Organised Stirling hadn't worked that out before she let her rage destroy everything? You're slipping, Jade. I always thought you were ten steps ahead of me, but I guess I was wrong. Maybe it was time for a new PA? Now, about that coffee?'

'No. Absolutely no! I've got three days before I have to go back to work. I'm still jet-lagged from the flight over, and I just want to rest. Get out of here before I call the police.'

'Be my guest, Jade. What are you going to tell them exactly? An old friend stopping by to visit isn't a crime,' he chuckled, 'but destroying someone's property, now that's another matter altogether.'

'Why are you doing this?'

'Why am I doing this? Why am *I* doing this? Jade, you started this game. If you want a truce, then just say so. Coffee?'

Jade stomped to the open-plan kitchen, unaware that behind a small door inside the pantry was a suitcase with all her clothing. Jade fumbled with the towel around her, and secured it tightly. The kettle boiled, and she set out the cafetiere and cups, and put some milk on the stove to heat. From time to time she looked up at him to see if it was true: Ashley Lyndhurst was here, in Australia, sitting just metres away from her while she made coffee. Each time she looked up, he had the same expression on his face: a cat with a mouse in the corner, flicking his tail and biding his time.

'Here's your coffee,' she said. 'I'm going to bed. Be gone by the morning.'

And, carrying her coffee in one hand, she picked up the other damp towel in the other and walked away.

'Not so fast, Jade.' He was behind her now. 'You're not going anywhere without me.'

'What are you talking about?'

'You owe me, remember?'

'Yes, but I don't...how on Earth do you expect me to repay you for the damage I caused.'

'I can think of a few ways,' he smiled, touching her shoulder.

'You've got to be joking! That's...that's akin to prostitution. I'm not...'

'Go to sleep, Jade. I'll just catch a few winks myself.'

'What? In here? In this bed? Why can't you sleep in the spare room?'

'Simple, really. I don't want to. And besides, I can make sure you don't escape if I stay in here.'

'Escape with nothing but a bath towel for cover? Give me a break!'

'No, Jade. Damn it! You give *me* a break. What the hell did I do to you? Haven't I been a good employer? Didn't I give you your own company car? How many PAs get one of those? A bloody convertible BMW! It's not even on a lease. I put it in your name. Please don't tell me you sold it.'

Jade looked down at the toenail polish on her toes. Wrong colour, she decided. Purple didn't really work. Next time she'd try red. Studying her toes some more, she nearly jumped out of her skin when Ashley yelled at her.

'You sold it? Jade! And your pension plan? It was generous. Plus you had double the annual leave of everyone else in the office. And your pay; you weren't exactly on minimum wage! You travelled everywhere with me. I would have bought you anything, Jade, anything. Did I ever yell at you? Did I mistreat you? Was I harsh? Did I exclude you from my business dinners at home or abroad? I even gave you a very generous clothing allowance. Correct me if I'm wrong, but I'm pretty sure it was double Emilia's annual salary. What the hell did I do wrong? Answer me that? Please. I would have given you everything. I don't know what else to do.' Ashley's hands were on her shoulders, and when he noticed her shaking he took the coffee cup from her hand and moved it over to the bedside table. 'Get some sleep,' he said, walking out of the room. Within seconds, he was back with his coffee cup.

'I'm not going anywhere, so don't even think of escaping.'

One sip of his coffee and he immediately spat it out. 'What the... *Jade!*'

'What's wrong?' she asked innocently. 'I thought I made the best coffee in the world.'

'You do... when you don't put salt in it!'

Ashley pulled back the covers, and stripped off his clothes, one item at a time. Jade watched his taut muscles, built up over years of 6am sessions in his home gym. It wasn't as if she hadn't seen him getting dressed before, but getting undressed while she wore next to nothing, disturbed every cell in her being.

Naked, he lay on the bed, then patted the space beside her. 'Come on, get some sleep.'

Jade looked at the body of God before her. Sleep? Was he joking? How could she sleep when the object of seven years of pent-up lust was lying in bed beside her?

'I... I've changed my mind. I don't think I'm that tired after all. Perhaps I'll go and read for a while.'

'Oh no you don't! Jade Stirling, with or without that damp towel around you, you're getting into this bed. Now.'

For the first time in seven years of pre-empting his every need, suddenly she was unsure of whether he was serious or joking.

'But I'm...'

'Jade. Bed. Now.'

'You're not the boss of me!' she yelled, finding her feet. 'No, I will not get into bed with you Ashley Lyndhurst.'

'Don't you find me attractive? Can you honestly say you've never fancied me being in your bed, Jade?'

'I want you to leave. I don't want you here. Not in this house, not in this bed, and most certainly not in my life. I'll find a way to pay you back, every last penny, but I am not doing it this way. Not ever. Now leave!'

'No. I'm not leaving. Answer my question, Jade. Do you find me attractive?'

'What a ridiculous thing to say! Every woman finds you attractive. Even blind women can see you coming. I'm no different to anyone else.'

'So you *do* fancy me in your bed?' he smiled.

'I didn't say that!'

'Jade, come to bed. Get some sleep. I promise I won't lay a hand on you, unless, of course, you change your mind.'

After ensuring the towel around her was secure, she tentatively moved onto the bed. Ashley pulled the sheet over them, and resisted the urge to kiss her. 'Sleep tight, Jade.'

'I doubt I'll sleep at all,' she whispered.

Ashley watched her body expand and collapse with each gentle breath until finally she was asleep. Could it be true? Did she really turn his world upside down because she felt something for him? Had he been so blind to her? How was that even possible? They spent six days a week together, rarely leaving each other's side. And every year, she worked through her annual leave not daring to leave him with another PA.

The Price of Love

While Jade slept, Ashley stole into the kitchen to ensure that her suitcase was out of view. First, he retrieved a skirt, matching blouse, underwear and some sandals. A small laugh escaped him when he realised that it was his money that had secured such stylish clothing. Then he remembered the last time she'd worn this skirt. They'd had lunch next to the Thames River. Ashley had just landed a huge contract for a major celebrity's worldwide concert tour, and took Jade out to celebrate away from the office. At the park, they sipped champagne and laughed until sunset. Jade had looked so beautiful, and he'd told her so in an employer-employee sort of way. Had she read too much into it? Ashley's mind raced to a million other memories. Perhaps he'd given her reason to believe that they had something special? Maybe it was all those dinners at the Ritz; all to celebrate contracts, of course, but perhaps they meant more to her? And then he recalled all the weekends on his yacht for a bit of R&R, and as a bonus for all her hard work. What about the hot air balloon ride in Devon on her birthday to celebrate their fifth anniversary of working together?

What an idiot he'd been! All these years of wanting to give her the best, and it was right there all along: she was far more than his PA. And somehow, in the process of trying to care for her, he'd turned her world upside down by insisting that she stay home in bed, rather than be by his side. It must have been a huge kick in the guts for her. And to go with Leonie? No wonder she was incandescent. Of the fifty staff at Lyndhurst Incorporated, Leonie Allan was one person that Jade had made quite clear did not fit in with the company. Ashley recalled no less than a dozen times when Jade suggested he pave the way for 'the bimbo' to join a new business and leave his company. Why hadn't he listened to her? If he had, they wouldn't be in this position now. Ashley was fighting with everything he had to win Jade back. Back to what? To be his PA? No, she deserved more than that. Could he give her a piloting job? Yes, he could, but then he'd never see her. The pilots for Lyndhurst Incorporated kept ridiculous hours. What would be the point of her being a London-based pilot if their paths rarely crossed?

Ashley slept on the sofa rather than go to bed; he knew that her warm naked body next to him was just asking for trouble. First and foremost, he was a man. There was no way he'd be able to keep his hands from touching her. The sofa was the only option.

At first light, he awoke to the cacophonous roar of Australian birds, not to mention withdrawal pangs for coffee.

When Jade woke up, Ashley greeted her with the aroma of coffee from freshly ground beans.

'Good morning. Thought I'd make you coffee for a change. Milk and unsweetened, right? No salt, I promise,' he smiled.

'Surprised you even know what I like or don't like,' she muttered, turning away from him.

Emilia was right: Jade *was* in love with him. How the hell was he going to woo her back to his company without leading her on?

'Maybe you need to tell me what you like, Jade,' he said kindly. 'Help me get to know you. All of you.'

'And why on Earth would I do that?' she snapped, sitting up to get out of bed. The towel fell to her waist.

'Damn it,' she said, pulling it up around her.

'Don't mind me. Nothing I haven't seen before.' He smiled.

'Can I have a bit of privacy please?'

Ashley couldn't help laugh at her irritation.

'I've never really seen this side of you before, Jade. You've always got everything so under control. Could it be that you're out of your comfort zone?'

'Of course I'm out of my comfort zone! My former boss, standing next to me, while I'm naked? Yes I'm out of my comfort zone. Where are my clothes?'

'Your comfort zone will be pleased to know that they're not cut into shreds, or soaked in red dye...'

'Ink. I told you. It's red ink.'

'Yes, ink. Ever the pedant, Jade. Ink! Your clothes are intact, and being well cared for. In fact, look what I have over here,' he said, pointing to the day's chosen items. 'Do you remember wearing that skirt by the river?'

'Of course I do. Why did you choose that?'

'I thought it might make you smile. A nice memory.'

'Every item of clothing I have reminds me of you, and it's probably time I got myself a new wardrobe!'

'But you don't have a wardrobe allowance anymore. You told Fred to cut it off, as I recall.'

'True, but I do have a job, and if you ever let me out of this place I can go back to earning money.'

'I'm not exactly holding you hostage, Jade. You're free to walk out that door.'

'Can I get dressed in privacy, then?'

'Actually, I rather fancy the view. It was a long night on the sofa,' he said as he brushed his hand through his hair. 'Here, let me pass you your clothes.'

And so he did, one item at a time, beginning with her lace panties and bra. There was a certain pleasure in watching her blush.

'I'm not getting dressed with you in the room, Ashley.'

'Why not? You've watched me get dressed countless times. Always there, weren't you, Jade? So reliable. Every morning, five days a week, choosing my tie, shirt, suit, even my socks. And casual clothes for Saturdays at the office. Beats me how I ever managed Sundays.'

'Well, you always had so much on your plate. The schedule is so hectic, that I just was trying to make your life easier.'

'Easier? It would have been easier if you didn't force me to sack my maid!

'Forgive me for feeling a bit jaded about a fifty-year-old Polish woman who only made you toast and sauerkraut every morning! That woman wasn't worth the money you paid her.'

'And you were?' he asked sarcastically.

'What?' she gasped. 'You never complained about the breakfasts I made you!'

'I loved your breakfasts, Jade, but you were my PA not my dresser or cook or housecleaner.'

'Well, why didn't you say something if having me around was such a chore!'

'Because...' he sighed deeply. And there it was: she won. What an idiot he'd been! For seven long years he was nothing but an idiot. 'Because it's never been a chore having you around. Not once. Not on any single day. Have I ever told you how much I hated Sundays?'

Their eyes met. 'You are a pleasure to have around. Well, you were. You always have been. The day you walked into my office for that interview, I was completely taken by you. It was like someone had put the Sun itself right into my office. You were such a stark contrast to the miserable weather outside the window. What can I do to win you back?'

'There is nothing to win back. This is my new life. I'm happy here. I don't want to go back to London, and I don't want to work for you. I have nothing else to say.'

And with those words, he left her alone in the bedroom. Not a word of reply. No goodbye. Ashley simply shut the door behind him.

Jade dressed slowly. Yes, of course she remembered the skirt, but not because of the river. No, it was something else. Ashley had seen her, on a lunch break, standing outside a little boutique admiring the skirt on the mannequin. Ashley had laughed at her, saying she shouldn't waste her half-hour break window shopping, and that she should be eating. But he'd caught a tear in her eye.

'Whatever is wrong?' he'd asked so compassionately.

'It's my 19th birthday, and I'm missing my family. The skirt reminded me of my mum. Silly, I know, but when I was a little girl she used to sew me skirts like this. It's such a simple, feminine style.'

'Why don't you buy it, then?' he'd asked.

'Girls like me don't buy clothes from boutiques like this,' she sniffed.

'Why not?'

Jade had merely raised her eyebrows at him. 'Best go and get myself some lunch. See you soon. Oh, do you want me to get you something while I'm out?'

'No, Jade. I'm quite capable of buying myself a bite to eat. Actually,' he said, passing her a £50 note. 'Bring some boxes of sushi from the little Japanese place when you've finished eating. We could have them for dinner while we take that conference call from the Houston office.'

Jade didn't know that he'd watched her walk away, and then looked at the skirt.

By the time she'd arrived back at her desk, there was a small packet wrapped in mauve tissue paper and ribbon, a bouquet of nineteen immaculate red roses, a hamper of chocolate and savoury treats, and a card which read: *Girls like you deserve the best! Happy birthday, Jade. Ash xx'* The following week, her pay packet included a clothing allowance.

From that day on, everyone knew Jade was something special. No one else in the office got birthday presents from Ashley Lyndhurst. Jade wondered if he remembered buying the skirt. It obviously meant far more to her than it did to him.

A knock on the front door of the bungalow startled Ashley, and he instantly leapt up to answer it. A handsome young blond man in a pilot's uniform, with the Roo Airlines logo, stood on the doorstep smiling. Ashley wondered if it was the man Tom had mentioned as having a fancy for Jade.

'Hi mate. Is Jade in?'

'Sure. Jade?' he called.

When Jade walked out of the bedroom, Ashley found himself back on the Thames with her, sipping champagne and laughing. This moment seemed surreal.

'Kev. Hi. What are you doing here?'

'Thought I'd pop by and see if you were free for dinner tonight, but I see you've already got company.'

'No I haven't. This is my former employer, Ashley Lyndhurst. Ash, this is Kev Peterson. Yes, I'm free. I'd love to come out with you.'

Ashley felt his blood boil. 'Actually, I think you've forgotten you had a prior engagement. Jade?' Ashley looked her in the eyes in a way which made it quite clear that she wasn't going anywhere with anyone but him.

'Can I take a rain check, Kev? Tomorrow night works for me if you're free,' Jade said.

Ashley realised she was trying to milk the situation for all it was worth.

'Yeah, that'd be great,' Kev replied.

'Actually, Jade. We have that little issue of, er, the Alfalfa and Ink merger to discuss.' Ashley turned to Kev. 'Sorry, I'm afraid you're out of luck this week. Her dance card is full.'

Kev left, and Ashley said 'Think I might take a shower, and then I'm going to take you out for lunch.'

Jade glared at him.

As soon as she heard Ashley in the shower, Jade marched to the kitchen and turned on the hot tap at full speed. Within seconds she heard him yell.

'A bit cold in that shower for you, buddy?' she said softly. And then she stepped into the toilet room and flushed it.

'Jeez, Jade!' he yelled, his voice booming through the rooms.

Then she casually walked back to the kitchen and let the hot water tap run. The man was making it impossible for her to think straight.

Ashley stormed out of the shower, and with nothing more than a towel around his waist, he walked up to her. 'Would it have been that hard to let me have a shower? I'm pretty jet lagged myself, you know?'

'No one stopped you having a shower!'

'I thought I knew you, Jade. But this whole Jade Unleashed vibe you've got going on is rather unsettling. I'll sack Leonie if it makes you happy. Anyone else you want me to fire?'

'I have a new life, Ashley. You're not part of it.'

'I'm here in your bedroom. I think that *does* make me part of your life.'

Jade could barely stand up as she watched him dry the rest of his body.

'Could you not have dried yourself in the bathroom?'

'You have a problem with me drying myself in here? What's wrong, Jade? Never seen a naked man before?'

'I really think…'

'Look, how do you want to play this, Jade? You can replace and pay for every last bit of damage to my property, and then you don't ever have to see me again or…'

'Or what?' she asked suspiciously.

After he hung the towel on a rail in the bathroom, he came back and stood before her completely naked.

Jade observed how his shoulders were broad and well-defined. As her eyes followed him down the length of his body, she felt her legs wobble at his toned abdominals.

The man was distracting!

'Can you please put some clothes on?' she asked.

'What clothes would they be? The scrap pile of

Savile Row suits shredded by a psycho? Sewing isn't my strong point, Jade!'

'You were saying?' she prompted him, averting her eyes.

'Marry me.'

'*What?*' As her eyes returned to him, she struggled to make eye contact. Ashley's physique was a work of art. Every muscle had her swooning. It was as if someone had sculpted him to perfection. It was impossible not to be taken in by the pure art of his body.

'Marry me. Two years, and then you're free. Debt paid.'

'Are you *crazy*?' she almost spat the words in his face. 'Marry you? Why?'

Ashley moved in closer to her, his dark, slightly wavy hair, damp and smelling of her citrus shampoo. He was so close now that she could feel the warmth rising from his body; so close, in fact, that she could almost lean over and kiss him.

'Crazy. Funny word that, Jade. Let me see. Did I cut thousands of pounds worth of fine, tailor-made, bespoke suits to shreds? Did I cover my floors in thousands of tiny seeds and sprout them into existence in a comfy bed of pure-wool carpet? Did I soak said carpet in water? Did I turn on the central heating and pretend my penthouse was a greenhouse? Did I dip ties in food dye...'

'In ink,' they said in unison.

'And you ask if I'm crazy?'

When he reached forward and pulled her unapologetically into his arms, she fell into his world within seconds. Jade felt the ache in his body, in his kisses. How had he never noticed her before?

Reluctantly, she pulled away.

'Why,' she gasped, trying to catch her breath, 'do you want to marry a crazy woman?'

'Two years, Jade. Two years as Mrs Lyndhurst and your debt will be wiped. You can walk away a free woman without any sense of being beholden.'

'I don't feel beholden to you!'

'Two years, Jade. It'll zip by.'

'But my job! I can't let Tom down.'

'You let me down. You had a contract. Two months notice.'

'Actually, Ash,' she said, using his abbreviation for the first time in seven years, 'here's the thing: when you asked me to retype the contract at our annual review, you didn't seem that interested about what was on there. Your exact words were: "write your dream contract". You should have read the small print, Ash.' She tut tutted.

Jade knew him well enough to sense that she was really starting to irritate him now.

'My contract actually says I don't have to give you any notice, though you were obligated to give me six months notice should my services no longer be needed. You signed off on it, Mr Lyndhurst.' The look on his face made it clear that he'd been outwitted. 'You know, for a businessman, you're pretty easy to pull the wool over.'

'Yes, you seem to know a lot about wool, don't you?'

If she thought she was having the last laugh, she was wrong. Within seconds Ashley picked her up and carried her to the bed. 'You owe me, Ms Stirling, and you can start paying your debt right now!'

'No, don't do this.'

'If you mean no, then stop looking at me like you

41

mean yes. If you mean no, then start explaining what you did to my home. They were not the actions of a woman who had no interest in me! You shouldn't have kissed me back like you wanted me to keep going. What is it, Jade? Yes or no? Tell me!'

'Let me go. I'll pay you back, every last penny, but I'm not paying you back like this. Not now. Not ever!'

'You can keep your job with Tom, but we'll come to an arrangement. One month here, and one month with me in the UK.'

'Why?'

'Why not? Have you got any better suggestions?'

'What do you get out of this?'

'A PA I can rely on. One who is irreplaceable, even if it means I only have her every other month.'

'Is that all?' her breathing was rapid and as he held her in his arms, she realised he showed no signs of letting her go.

'And full conjugal rights.'

'Con…*what*?'

'It's hardly a marriage, Jade, if I don't have the pleasure of sleeping with you. And I'm sure it would be a pleasure,' he smiled.

'That's not marriage. It's prostitution!'

'Hardly. No cash would be exchanged. We'll just consider it services rendered. Obviously I'd pay you for your PA work, and any flights you piloted. I'd reinstate your clothing allowance, and…'

'You'd let me *fly*?'

'Yes, Jade. I'd let you fly. I should have offered you a position as soon as you qualified. I'm sorry,' he said, his hand touching her cheek softly.

'Tom won't say yes to this,' she said firmly.

'Tom owes me. He has no choice.'

'What do you mean? How come the whole world bows at your feet?'

'Must be my charm,' he laughed. Before she could reply, he lifted off her blouse, and then pulled down her skirt. Jade showed no sign of resistance, and moaned as Ashley slowly let his hand smooth its way along the curve of her back. The explosive heat between them caught them both off guard. As his kisses played upon her shoulder, Jade could feel him fight against his instinct. Ashley's lips traced their way slowly down her body, and as she raised herself up off the bed, desperate to become one with him, she reacted involuntarily to his every touch; spasms of pleasure torturing her in the most exquisite of ways. From time to time she looked up at him, and watched the pleasure on his face. Oh yes, he was under her spell. A red-blooded woman had been at his side for the past seven years, a woman he'd mentally put brackets around, and now she beckoned him closer with each movement. Jade wanted him inside of her. Now.

When he fought against his body's drive, and rolled over beside her, Jade sighed with disappointment. Did he just smile?

Ashley wondered if he should stand up and walk away now or consume Jade and leave her senseless? If he made love to her, then there'd be no way she'd stay in Australia.

As tempted as he was to walk away, damn it, he was a man! And her body was calling for him to do the right thing. Ashley's fingers traced her abdomen and then her hips before finally easing their way between her thighs. Jade might have said she wanted him out of her life, but her body was telling a different story.

Ashley felt her burning up for him with potent desire. Finally he entered her to the sound of her sighing with pure delight, and accompanied her satisfied sounds with a guttural groan. Whatever his motivations for getting her into bed, it had backfired. Ashley wanted her as desperately as she wanted him. Later, he'd deal with managing his rampant lust . For now, he had a job to do and he listened to her moans: low and deep and unrestrained; her breathing raw and ragged. Like the ticking of a clock, her body pulsed every second with a deep thud between her legs. The only way to stop the bomb was to diffuse the tension.

'I need you Ashley. I need you inside me.' The desperation on her face was priceless. 'I need you!'

Ashley removed himself from her, and got up from the bed.

'That was highly inappropriate of me. I'm your boss. I shouldn't be...'

'No you're not! You're not my boss!'

Ashley turned away so she couldn't see the smile on his face. It had taken enormous will to get off that bed. One thing was for sure: she was worth waiting for. After a moment, he came down and put his arms around her.

When Ashley flew to Australia to bring his PA back to London, it hadn't occurred to him that he'd want to make love to her, let alone propose!

'Why did you get jealous when Kev came by to ask me out?' she asked softly, as he stroked her hair. 'He's just a pilot at Roo Airlines. End of story.'

'No Jade, it's not the end of the story. It's just the beginning. He's not right for you. You've been here for less than a week and already you have men calling on you.'

'Well, I didn't have time for gentlemen callers in my previous job!'

'Would you have wanted them?'

When she didn't answer, Ashley wondered what she was thinking. Not for a second did he realise that her one thought was: *I only ever wanted you.* I wanted you to notice me. To *see* me. To see me as more than the hired help.

'We've always had a good relationship, Jade. The boundaries were blurred. I can see that now. I asked too much of you, and you were always so willing to bend over backwards for me. We spent too much time together; too many nights in foreign hotels and late-night dinners. Too many glasses of champagne while travelling in first-class luxury. If my demands were a problem, why didn't you say? I'd have listened.'

'The more I gave, the more you wanted. I turned my whole life on its axis to be what you needed. But it wasn't enough.'

'What are you talking about?' he asked, pulling her in closer to him. 'You've always been enough for me. Always. How can I make it up to you?' Ashley kissed her again, softly this time.

'I thought I was supposed to be making it up to you? Debt-ridden for two years, as I recall.'

'So, you'll marry me then?' he asked, his face lighting up.

'No. No I won't marry you Ashley Lyndhurst. If I ever marry, it will be for love, and love only. I'll marry because the man in question wants me more than he wants life itself! I'll marry because he can't breathe without me. I'll marry because someone deems me worth their every waking thought, and not because I sprinkled a few alfalfa seeds on the floor.'

'A few seeds? Right now I have twenty thousand pounds of pure wool carpet being ripped out of my home.'

'There's a lot to be said for wooden flooring,' she smirked, but he didn't let her off so lightly when she attempted to laugh. Although she kept her eyes poker-like, he sensed she was suppressing a laugh.

'I'd have given anything to see the final product,' she said.

'You think it's funny, don't you? Don't worry, I kept a photographic record for the police,' he said, wiping the smile off her face.

Of all the people in his life, surely she knew his home was his haven from a hectic work schedule, and that despite being in the heart of London, it was his sanctuary? And he had trusted her fully with his home!

Ashley allowed her the luxury of laughing, but he also knew when enough was enough. If it hadn't cost so much money, he'd probably be laughing out loud too.

'Why alfalfa?'

'I thought the sight of the colour jade would be a visual reminder of what you'd be missing. How was your two-week holiday with Ms Allan?'

'Holiday? You know damn well it was a business trip. For me, anyway. You were right. That woman has no place in my company. No place at all. Does she do anything besides text her friends and paint her toenails?'

'You tell me...I've only been telling you every day for the past five years that she was unsuitable.'

'Actually Jade, *twice* a day, every day, for the past five years.'

'So why didn't you listen to me? You listen to me about everything else.'

'Tell me, Jade. If you could turn back time to just

46

before you came down with a cold, what would you do differently?'

Ashley hoped for an apology or some sort of easy truce between them. Would she try and redeem herself for such spiteful behaviour?

'What would I do differently? Easy. I'd notch the central heating up another five degrees!'

'Jesus, Jade! I'm giving you a chance to apologise. Don't dig the hole any deeper!'

'From where I'm standing, I'm not the one in the hole. No one on the planet needs a PA this badly. Hannah's a sweet girl. I'm sure it won't be long until she's choosing your ties and poaching your eggs."

'I don't want Hannah. I want…I want you!' There. He said it. That was the truth: he wanted Jade.

'Too bad. Hannah's on a five-year contract to be your PA.'

'What?'

'Amazing, isn't it? Bless her, she couldn't believe it either. Five years with the wonderful, charming, highly respected Ashley Lyndhurst. Every girl's dream. All that financial security; she's one happy girl. I'm sure she'll *please* you.'

'Jade, is there anything else I should know about? Any other nasty little surprises?'

'Hmmmm. Can't think right now. I'll let you know if I remember. Look, Ash, I've got two days off work. I need my clothes. I need my spare pilot's uniform. Help me out here. Where are my clothes?'

'I'll help you out!' Ashley wanted to be furious with her, but damn it, he couldn't. What he really wanted was to have her back in his arms.

This time he wasn't going to walk away. Every primal urge to devour her coursed through his veins.

When his lips once again shadowed hers, they drank in the pleasure of each other's bodies. Jade's skin was smooth as silk beneath his fingers, and the sweet scent of arousal lingered from their earlier explorations. It lured him to the furthest reaches of her body. Ashley was stirred into full force as he kissed his way from the nearly invisible down on her ear lobes, across her soft breasts and down, down, down to her private temptation. Kisses lined her curvaceous hips, and his hands pushed her toned legs apart.

'Relax,' he whispered. 'You can enjoy this all you like. It's not as if the neighbours can hear us.'

Jade made the sounds of a woman in ecstasy. It was too much; the sensation too intense.

Ashley found it pleasurable gratifying her in this way, and her non-verbal noises urged him on.

'Don't you dare walk away this time!' she moaned.

He laughed, and said 'I'll try not to!'

When he decided that she was near to tipping over that glorious edge of ecstasy into oblivion, he pulled away.

'But you promised!' she pleaded.

'Did I?' he chuckled, and before she could answer, his strong, virile length was inside her; slowly at first, while he found a rhythm she could adjust to, and then as he noticed a tear in the corner of her closed eye, it occurred to him that this was probably her first time. You idiot! he told himself, then paused and kissed her cheek.

'I hope I didn't hurt you.'

Jade's eyelashes fluttered until her eyes opened, then closed as she luxuriated in her drunken reverie. 'I'm fine. Just fine.'

Although Ashley instinctively wanted to quickly satisfy the intense detonation which needed to take place between them, something had changed. There was no way he could do that now. They weren't meeting each other as equals in lovemaking. He was experienced, and she wasn't; he had to meet her half way. No, damn it. He had to do better than that! Ashley Lyndhurst had to go back to the starting line and hold her hand.

'Are you okay?' she asked.

'Perfectly. I want to savour every second with you. I'll never get this day again.'

When he met the smile on her lips with a kiss so exquisitely soft and succulent, that she moaned as if she might die from the beauty of their connection, he hoped that she'd consider two years more of this would be worth giving up her job with Roo Airlines.

Ashley had never made love so slowly in his life, but far from being frustrating it had the opposite effect: on both of them! Sensations of bliss were agony in their intensity. Neither of them had ever experienced such concentrated ecstasy. Elation led them, through glacially slow plunges in the hot spring of her hidden cavern, to dizzying heights. Legs shaking, hearts pounding, sighs of satiation had them both teetering at the edge, wondering what the future would bring.

'Reckon that debt must be just about paid by now, Mr Lyndhurst.'

'Not by a long way. I'm starting to wonder if two years was a severe underestimate. Perhaps twenty years would be more suitable?'

'Twenty?' was the last thing she had to say, and then she cried out into the afternoon air. And with one final thrust they urgently exploded. *Falling, falling, falling…*

A kookaburra laughed outside her window as if to say 'You haven't even begun to pay your debt!'

They lay in bed for some time. Words were unnecessary. They'd entered a new world, one from which they'd never return. And now they were here, there was no roadmap, no Google search to show them the way out or which direction to go. Finally, Ashley kissed her on the forehead, and then stood up. Her looked down at her deliciously satisfied body, feeling rather pleased with himself. Consumed. Sated. As he watched her, Ashley realised that she didn't know what her body was capable of, and smiled.

'I think we could both do with going out for a meal. We've used up rather a lot of calories this afternoon, though I have to admit it was a pleasant diversion. I'm going to take a shower. Jade, don't mess with the hot water. If you do,' he smiled, 'we'll be going straight back to bed. I'll leave it to you to decide what you're more hungry for: me or food.'

Jade had another idea. As soon as she heard the water sprays, she wrapped a towel around herself and logged onto her laptop. All the office passwords were still filed on there. Everything in her body told her it was wrong, but…she just couldn't help herself. Ashley Lyndhurst was far too smug for her liking. And how dare he come to Australia and…make love to her as if she was his.

The afternoon had been everything she'd always dreamed of, his kisses like maple syrup, and caresses so tender. If only…if *only* he cared for her in the way she did for him. Everything would be just perfect. Well, apart from the little issue of his carpet and clothing.

Firstly, she logged into Emilia's email simultaneously throwing up a silent prayer to the Gods:

50

please let her forgive me, I know not what I do.

```
TO: Ashley Lyndhurst
Dear Mr Lyndhurst
I've been unsuccessful at reaching you on
your mobile. We've got a situation in the
office, and I don't know how to handle it.
Require your urgent return to London.
Regards, Emilia.
```

Jade sat back in her chair. 'That's my work done for the day,' she said out loud. 'Hang on a minute, no it's not.' Stifling the emerging giggles, she promptly signed out of Emilia's office email and logged into Leonie's account.

```
TO: Ashley Lyndhurst

Ash...
```

Jade wanted to type 'she purred', but that would have been kind of a giveaway!

```
Thank you so much for the fabulous fortnight
away. We really must 'do it' again. I
haven't stopped thinking about you. The
way you smell of coffee, and what is that
aftershave? Oh my, it makes me think all
sorts of naughty things about you. How
did you ever decide on such an erotically
scented cologne? Anyway, just wanted to say
'hi', and I can't wait to see you again.
Oh, I don't think Hannah's the right fit
for you. Perhaps I could be your new PA?
```

We were such a good team, don't you think?
Love, Leonie. xxxxxxxxxxxxxxxxxxxxxxxxx

The shower was still running. Tempting as it was to run the hot water, just once for fun, this was far more rewarding. Now, who else might need to email their boss?

Oh yes. The lovely Hannah. Sweet, five-year-contract, fumbly-mumbly Hannah.

TO: Ashley Lyndhurst

Dear Sir
I hope you're enjoying your trip to Australia. I just wanted to let you know that I revamped your office. All those pot plants were starting to look a bit worse for wear so I disposed of them. Did you know there were fifteen palms in there? Who needs fifteen palms in their office? Anyway, it feels much clearer in there now.

I've converted the filing system to the Hannah Special. That means things are filed in date order rather than subject or alphabetical order. I like chronological systems. I'll teach it to you when you get back, if you like.

Oh, and one more thing. The carpet in your penthouse... well, turns out, the flooring is going to need some time to dry and that you won't be able to live there on your return. They mentioned 'several months'. When I said that you wouldn't be happy about it, Leonie Allan (from Human Resources) offered for you to stay in her home for a while. Isn't that so kind?

Oh, and one more thing: Axel Duff said he's coming on Friday to sign the contract. He said he wanted Jade to be there or it was a no-go. I didn't know what to say. Is Jade coming back?

Oh, and one more MORE thing: there's a small betting group in force here at the office. Fifty to one says you can't bring Jade back.

Can you pat a kangaroo for me? Do they bounce down the streets? I always wanted a kangaroo.

Oh, and one more, more MORE thing...Oh, I can't remember what it is. Shoot, I really can't remember! Ooops, kettle is boiling. Coffee time.

Ashley stood in the shower, willing the cold water to erase all signs of his arousal. 'Down, boy, down. It's crazy to want her again so soon,' he told himself. Nothing he did could get rid of the image of her beneath him: beautiful, vulnerable, hungry for him. Jade had quivered like an Autumn leaf at his every touch, and her body moaned, ached, whimpered and sighed. Before he got out of the shower, he had to make sure he could think straight.

When she heard the shower stop, Jade signed out and flicked down the lid of her laptop. Within seconds she put it inside the writing bureau and pulled down the accordion-style desk lid. When Ashley walked into the room, with just a towel around him, she gave him her brightest smile.

'So, a spot of lovemaking puts you in a good mood, does it?' He laughed.

You've no idea, mate. One thing was clear: she was determined to make him pay for abandoning her in London and taking Leonie in her place. Oh yes, she'd make him pay for a long time.

'Coffee?'

'No, Jade. I'll have some after dinner.'

Something about her was different. Ashley couldn't quite put his finger on it. In no time at all, she'd gone from feisty to friendly. It was unnerving. What the hell was she up to?

As he looked her up and down, he whispered 'I remember buying you that skirt.'

'You do?'

'It was your nineteenth birthday, and you were crying. Missing your mum, you said. I could see that you coveted that skirt like nothing else on Earth. What I didn't know when I bought it for you was that you'd wear it to work for the next three weeks straight. Everyone thought it was your new uniform!'

'I love this skirt.'

'I know. It was made for you.'

'I didn't know you remembered.'

'Jade, I remember everything.'

Life was far easier and less complicated when they were strictly employer and employee. They could never go back there again. Everything had changed. Everything!

'I could do with some other clothes if we're going out to dinner. Most of my clothes are in transit.'

'No problem. We can buy something on the way.'

'That's really not necessary.'

'My bride-to-be deserves the best, so that's what she shall have.'

'Ashley...'

'Like I said, if you've got a better suggestion, then let me have it. I'll get dressed, and then we can head on our way.'

'I'll have a quick shower first.'

Twenty-five minutes later Jade walked into the lounge room and watched Ashley sitting at his laptop. The look on his face told her everything she needed to know.

'Something wrong?' she asked, using every bit of resilience to refrain from laughing.

'No,' he said, closing down the laptop. 'No, everything's just fine. Just fine. Are you ready?'

'Sure am,' she smiled broadly. Curiosity was killing her. Jade was desperate to ask why he was a bit on edge. Any interesting emails? she was keen to ask, but she bit her tongue. They made small talk about the weather, and Australian culture.

The taxi driver drove them to Balmain, in the inner city, and Jade spent an hour in Leona Edmiston's boutique. The first item she chose was a limited-edition floral frock, and Ashley urged her to buy several more pieces to tide her over while her wardrobe sailed from London to Australia.

'Just a few pairs of jeans will do. Mostly I'll be in my uniform. There's no point in having all these.'

'Humour me, Jade. You owe me, remember?'

'Okay.' You want humouring, she thought, I'll humour you.

Eight dresses, three winter coats, four handbags and six pairs of shoes later, she turned to him and asked 'Feeling humoured?'

'Deliciously so,' he said, meeting her eye.

'Emma Attenborough Hair and Makeup, how can I help you?'

'This is Ashley Lyndhurst, I spoke to someone earlier about scheduling in my fiancée for an appointment.'

'Yes, Mr Lyndhurst. We can see her in fifteen minutes.'

'I don't know how you did that. How kind, Mr Lyndhurst,' Jade smiled.

'Only the best for my fiancée.'

Their eyes met. Cat and mouse. Never before had she felt this amount of two-way tension between them. There had been moments, plenty of moments, when she wondered if he'd felt the same way, but always, *always*, he pulled back, changed the subject, left the room. Not now. Right here, the air could be cut. Everything about their lives had changed.

After an hour and a half in hair and makeup, Jade emerged.

'Wow.' That's all he said when she walked into the café where he'd been waiting. Jade noted that he said wow several times over the next half hour, and remained monosyllabic all the way to the restaurant.

If I keep wowing him, maybe I won't have to work off this debt, she wondered, but then something stabbed her in the chest. Jade rather liked the idea of spending the next two years as Mrs Lyndhurst. What she didn't like, not one bit, was the idea of all the years beyond that: *all those years of being the ex-Mrs Lyndhurst*. And as her face fell to match her mood, Ashley noticed.

'Jade, what's wrong? What's happened?'

Jade forced herself to perk up, and met his eyes with her brightest Monday-morning-at-the-office smile. 'Nothing at all.'

Ashley knew her well enough—revenge tactics aside—to know that something had changed. For the life of him, he couldn't figure out what had happened. One moment, she appeared to have enjoyed spending his money in the boutique; and the next, she looked ravishing when she came out of the salon. To his mind, she was pretty darn gorgeous before she entered, but there was nothing in their conversation that made him twig to why she looked so crestfallen.

Ashley linked his arm with hers, and carried her shopping spree in his other hand, then hailed a taxi. He decided not to intrude on the silence, but instead held her hand and gently rubbed it from time to time just to remind her that he was there. Perhaps asking her to marry him wasn't the best idea in the world. Maybe demanding she pay him back was the last straw. The honourable thing would be to let her stay in Australia, and for him to go back to London and look for a new PA. But this wasn't about a PA. Of course he could find a new one. Not Hannah! Not Hannah and her new filing system, god forbid! No, this was about Jade. Ashley could never find a new Jade Stirling. The world was only big enough for one of her.

Before long, they pulled up at Cockle Bay Wharf outside *Sepia*, a corporate-luxe restaurant.

Once seated, Ashley chose an eclectic wine to complement the first-class menu. The atmosphere fitted the restaurant's namesake: sepia-tinted art-deco design, with the central area dominated by a brass and marble bar.

The dim lighting accentuated the intimate atmosphere with its hidden nooks offering secret worlds away from the world.

The black and white floors were like a dance stage for the elegant waiting staff as they waltzed around attending to everyone's needs.

In silence, Ashley and Jade looked over the menu: contemporary cuisine with a Japanese twist by no less than a Tetsuya-trained chef.

'We should get married here, in Sydney, this month.'

Jade nearly spat her wine across the table. 'What's the hurry?'

So was that why she'd been so sullen? Was she terrified of the prospect? Ashley knew he had to play his cards carefully.

'Like I said Jade, if you have a more viable option to pay off this debt, then just say so.'

The helpless look on her face made him wonder if it was all worth it.

'I didn't think you had a better plan. Tell me, would it be that awful to be Mrs Lyndhurst? Most people already think we're married anyway.'

'But we're not.'

'No, we're not.'

Emilia was right: Jade was in love with him. So why wouldn't she just admit it?

'Wasn't this afternoon pleasant enough for you Jade? Was I not a good enough lover for your tastes?'

'What? What are you talking about? I...I...er...'

'Would two years of making love with me be that awful?'

'No! No it wouldn't be awful. It just wouldn't be...'

'Wouldn't be, what? What wouldn't it be, Jade?'

'It doesn't matter. You wouldn't understand.'

'Try me.'

Ashley watched as she fiddled with her dessert: caramelised apple with house-made clotted cream, malted meringues, salted buckwheat toffee, muscovado blackcurrant and sorrel leaves.

'It's just that...well, two years of my life is a huge amount of time to give to someone who doesn't love me. I don't want to just have sex with a man. I want it to mean something. I want to be loved.' There, she said it. At last.

Ashley wondered what to do with the way she'd so vulnerably lay her feelings right there on the linen tablecloth ready for him to scoop up. Would he pummel them right then and there, or would he nurture them like a tiny shoot?

Ashley surveyed the dessert he'd chosen: Hachiya persimmon, coconut yoghurt, salted-goat-milk sorbet, shichimi-pepper ganache, chocolate-crumb, coconut meringue with rum and milk jelly.

What he said next would make all the difference, and he knew that he had to get it right. Stalling for time, he savoured several mouthfuls, then wiped his lips with the napkin and looked up at her.

'You don't think I could grow to love you, Jade?' His voice was low, raspy. It felt unfamiliar to him.

'I can't answer that for you, Ashley. All I know is that I don't want to be a trophy bride or debt-ridden to you. I want...it doesn't really matter what I want, does it!' she said, crumpling the napkin up on the dessert plate.

'You are very loveable, Jade Stirling. I am even coming to find your revenge tactics rather...let's say, amusing. Charming in a jilted-by-the-"blind-to-the-obvious"-boss sort of way.'

'I am?'

'I have no doubt that I could fall in love with you, if that's what *you* want.'

'Really? But...but what do you want?'

'Whatever makes you happy.' Ashley's hand reached over to hers, and he lifted it up and kissed it softly. 'Whatever makes you happy.'

Jade bit her lip then asked 'Don't suppose you'd just write off the debt then, and we could go our separate ways?'

Was she really trying to wheedle her way out of this ludicrous marriage plan?

'Is that what you truly want, Jade? Do you want me to walk away? Do you want to spend the rest of your life never seeing me again?'

'I'm tired. Can we go home now?'

Despite his spotlight questioning, she managed to evade him.

'Well, actually, I've booked us a suite at Shangri La. I thought it would be nice to formally begin this liaison with a fresh start. Shall we go?'

'A hotel?'

'Yes, but not just any hotel, Jade. Only the best for my fiancée, as I said. You are still my fiancée, aren't you?'

Ashley watched the lump in her throat rise and fall. Was she having doubts?

'I don't want to be a divorcee. That's not part of my life's plan. I don't want to fail at something as important as marriage.'

Now he was getting somewhere. She *did* want to be married, she just didn't want to be divorced. But did she want to be married to him: Ashley Lyndhurst?

'We should probably take one day at a time, Ms Stirling.'

Jade surveyed the night-time skyline from their suite: the Opera House and the harbour bridge, majestic beneath the city lights. A light knock on the door caught her attention. Ashley answered to the sound of a firm voice calling: "Room service".

Jade looked over as a silver trolley was wheeled into the room. A beautiful bouquet of Singapore orchids and a bottle of champagne on ice were a visual prelude to the night before her.

Ashley tipped the young man, and closed the door behind him.

'Flowers for my beautiful fiancée,' he said, placing them on the bedside table.

As he poured the champagne into crystal flutes, he ventured a toast: 'To us. To our future as Mr and Mrs Lyndhurst.'

Just as Jade was about to take a sip, she looked him right in the eye. 'Are you sure you want this? There must be a woman in your life who's waiting for you?'

'Jade, you know as well as I do that you keep any potential date a full ten miles away from me with a simple look of those chocolate-coloured eyes of yours. Every woman in London is scared to come close to me!' he laughed, running his fingers through his dark, slightly wavy hair.

'Really?' she acted genuinely surprised.

'Jade Pitbull, was how Leonie once described you.'

'Perhaps we should toast to Leonie then? Heard from her lately?'

'Should I have?' he frowned. 'I'm not seeing her Jade. Surely you must know that. She's not my type by a long shot!'

'What is your type?' The words felt like an explosive as they came out of her mouth; like they might tear her world apart to hear the truth.

'My type? Let's see, Jade. You know me better than anyone else on this planet. What type do you think I'd be attracted to?'

Jade turned away from him and focused instead on the exquisite décor and breathtaking views.

'Honestly, I don't think you have a type. I think you could have any woman you wanted. All you'd have to do is snap your fingers. Hell, you don't even have to do that. Women just fall at your feet.'

'Answer the question, Jade. What is my type? Not who'd fall at my feet, but at whose feet would I fall?'

'I don't know,' she flustered. 'All I know is that you...you're kind, generous-hearted, and you're driven. You need someone who will love you and care for you and give you the freedom to follow your dreams.'

'What is my type, Jade?'

'I don't know!'

'You do know. You know everything about me. You've spent seven years caring for me and giving me the freedom to follow my dreams. You wait on me hand and foot. You know what I need before I do. You know how to calm me down when I'm ready to explode. You make me laugh when I think the day can't get any worse. You brighten up every board meeting. You bring me my favourite meals at lunchtime, and when I let you off work early enough, you have a beautiful meal waiting in my kitchen. There isn't anything you won't do for me. What am I looking for in a woman? Jade?'

'I don't know! I wish I knew, but I don't!' Tears slipped down her cheeks. 'I don't know what you want. I don't know.'

Immediately, his arms were around her.

'You do know. Jade, you do know what my type is.'

'I'm just jet-lagged still,' she cried into his chest. 'I'm sorry. I really need to get some sleep. It's been exhausting having you around. This wasn't how I was planning to spend my time off!'

'Don't start getting feisty on me again, Jade. It's too exhausting for both of us. Come to bed.'

Jade followed him as he carried the champagne to their bedside, and then turned to face her.

'I'll be a good husband to you, Jade. I promise. Just two years, and then you can walk away.'

Her face fell, like a crumpled fairy all collapsed in its little dress.

'If you want to...' he added.

Jade looked up at him. 'If I want to?'

'If you decide that being married to me suits you, then we don't have to divorce.'

'What? But....but you have a whole life to live. You'll want to find someone one day and really get married, and have children. You won't want to be tied to your former PA.'

'Here's an idea: why don't you help me find 'the one'? And until then, we can enjoy each other's company.

Win, win? For now, let's get to know each other some more,' he said, his fingers tracing her neckline. 'It feels like months since I've seen you naked.'

'It's only been about twelve hours...' her breath was ragged; she knew what was coming next.

'Hours. Are you sure? It feels like months,' and he swooped down on her lips.

'I'm tired,' she said, biting her lip nervously.

'Fine. I'm not going to force myself on you. If you don't desire me, Jade, then I don't imagine this marriage is going to work.'

'I didn't say that!'

'You do...'

'Of course I do. What red-blooded woman wouldn't?'

'Why don't you have a hot shower? It'll relax you before you go to sleep.'

Jade entered the bathroom, and flicked on the shower switch then caught her reflection in the mirror: flushed cheeks, watery eyes, arousal written all over her. *Cheat!* She told herself. *You couldn't be more obvious if you tried.*

No sooner had she stepped under the jet spray when Ashley entered the room. *Naked.* Completely naked. Her breath caught. So much for a relaxing shower, she thought. There was no way he wasn't going to step under that stream of steamy spray with her. As she admired every inch of him: his dark wavy hair and strong jawline to his virile torso, she wondered if he could tell that the anticipation was reciprocated. Did he have any idea that her knees were about to give way? That she had no way of supporting herself against the cocktail of hormones seeping through her bloodstream.

Jade looked exquisite; the water cascaded over

her shoulders, forcing her long dark hair to slink back against her scalp and shoulders, clinging to her as if she was the only thing in the world. If only she knew that Ashley suddenly realised that all he wanted was Jade. That's all he'd wanted for as long as he could remember. Until now, he'd just never let it come to the forefront of his mind; had never put it into words.

From the first day Jade walked into his office, full of confidence, he wanted her by his side. Just minutes before they met, he'd been notified that he'd lost two contracts. The day couldn't have got any worse, but in a matter of moments something had changed. The light way she talked, her enthusiasm for the aviation industry, the lessons she was taking. Life changed that day, but he didn't know how much it would change. If he'd been able to see into the future, been able to see that she was everything he'd ever need, he'd probably have taken her that day in the office even though she was eighteen years old.

It was no secret around Lyndhurst Incorporated that she was his favourite staff member. More than once, rumours circulated that something must have been going on, but the truth was he simply liked her company. Jade made every day easy, no matter what was on the agenda.

Ashley stepped under the shower spray with her, his hands holding her hips. 'You look beautiful,' he murmured. 'Absolutely beautiful.'

'So do you,' she said, running her fingers across his strong shoulders. 'I'm sorry for everything. I'm sorry about…your carpet.'

'And?'

'And your suits.'

'And?'

'The ties...'

'And?'

'And what? That's the full extent of my crimes, Mr Lyndhurst!'.

'And?' he continued.

'What? What else have I done?'

'Are you sorry for making me desire you so much?'

'I haven't made you desire me.'

'Oh yes you have!' Ashley kissed her again, and when they both came up for air he repeated the truth: 'Yes you have.'

'You've chosen it all by yourself...'

Ashley hoisted her up against the shower tiles, and lifted her legs around his hips. They weren't going anywhere. Right now, right here, he desired her more than anything in the world.

'I want to make love to you, Jade. May I?'

'You mean, you're actually asking my permission? What happened to your conjugal rights?' She threw the words at him, dismembering the intense chemistry that had built up under the head of the shower.

'We're not married yet, and yes, I'm asking your permission. I always will. Can I make love to you Jade?'

The look on his face was desperate. This wasn't about sex, or having his way with her. *What was it?* For seven years Jade had pre-empted his every need, and now, for the first time he was fully aware of it.

'Ash, I would love you to make love to me. Just like this morning. Yes. Yes please.'

And so, without waiting a second longer, they explored each other's bodies to completion. Exhausted, satisfied, shaking, he lifted her in his arms, turned off the shower, and carried her to bed. Now she could go to sleep; if she wanted to.

In-flight Troubles

They stayed at Shangri La a second night, and then headed back to Tom's bungalow in the Blue Mountains so Jade could get dressed for work. More than once she wondered if she'd be able to keep her eyes open; she'd barely slept since Ashley arrived back in her life.

It wasn't a long flight: Sydney to Melbourne, to take some big-wig celebrity to see his latest lover. But there was no doubt, in her exhausted condition, that it could be the longest flight of her life.

Jade's body tingled as if it had been pummelled into submission in the most beautiful way possible. No longer did her thoughts revolve around work or her ambition to set up her own flying school. The only thing she could think of was: Ashley Lyndhurst.

Ashley's baritone voice.

Ashley's touch.

Ashley's laugh.

Ashley. Ashley. Ashley! Damn it!

As soon as she tried to close her eyes, for even a second, his face was there: that strong jawline which made her feel safe; those deep-green eyes that reminded her of a dark forest filled with secrets; his shoulders, firm and muscular. Ashley's dark, slightly wavy, short hair, and how her fingers loved to slowly caress his head. How he smelled of spice and good coffee. No, she couldn't think straight at all. Jade's body was alive as if it had been awoken for the first time, and now had a mind of its own. It was as if she was in a constant state of arousal, and she didn't know how to turn the switch off!

Fearful that she wouldn't concentrate well enough to fly, she considered asking Tom for a day off.

Ashley pre-empted her plans, and phoned Tom to ask if he could co-pilot.

'Sure mate, just don't distract her.'

Seven years of watching Jade in business clothes, and today, dressed in her pilot's uniform, she looked just as gorgeous as ever with her wavy chocolate hair partially restrained into a pony tail, and her understated makeup. Jade Stirling had the look of a woman who'd been well loved, and it pleased her no end. Ashley had done that to her. His hands, and his hands alone, had calmed down the vengeful vixen. Never again would she contemplate any sort of revenge. No, not now. Ashley had Jade just where he wanted her, she realised, in the palm of his seductive hand. With every ounce of effort she could muster, Jade tried not to think of him undressing her, and discarding her pilot's uniform on the floor of the cabin.

Jade took a few deep breaths and tried to think of the roses in her mother's garden, hoping it would send her thoughts flying in another direction, but their scent only made her think of how good Ashley always smelled.

They climbed into the cockpit and Jade took control of the space. Firstly, she called to the flight controller, and confirmed that she was five minutes from preparing to drive onto the runway.

Jade looked at the clock on her console. It was in Greenwich Meantime. She looked at the watch on her left wrist, and noted Sydney time.

The low-voltage warning light alerted her to trouble. The engine didn't appear to be getting enough electricity.

'We need an engineer. I'm not taking anyone up in this until it's looked at.'

'Good call, Jade.' Ashley said.

Jade had her wits about her, even though she was utterly exhausted. If it had been one of his pilots coming to work on no sleep, she knows he'd probably have fired them. But he could hardly do that to Jade. Firstly, she no longer worked for him; secondly, *he* was the cause of her exhaustion. That it was only to be a short flight was her only consolation. Ashley offered, once again, to fly the plane; but the look on her face made it quite clear he should back off.

Jade apologised to her passenger, the great RT Hennit. Not that she thought he was great. *Philandering creep*, was her informed opinion. It wasn't the first time she'd been aware of him flying to a rendezvous and cheating on his wife while she stayed home with their triplets. The man always used Lyndhurst Incorporated when in Europe, and it had been Jade's job to ensure the pilots met his needs.

If there was anything that was bound to get Jade worked up, it was a man being unfaithful to his wife. *A crime punishable by death*, she once said to the girls in the office.

'Can you at least bring in some more alcohol? And how long is that going to take? I've got an appointment!'

'Better to be late than dead on time, Mr Hennit,' she said firmly. 'The engineer is coming over now.'

When she returned to the cockpit, Ashley met her with a coffee.

'I'm sorry. It was unfair of me to keep you awake all night. You shouldn't be flying.'

'I'll be fine. Once this baby is up in the air, we'll be landing just over an hour later. It's no problem. Honestly, Ashley, it's only 880 kilometres.'

'And the return flight?'

'Hennit isn't returning until tomorrow night. I can stay in a B&B and get some sleep. You can stay there, too,' she smiled, grateful for his company.

Ashley sat back in his seat, and closed his eyes.

'Bloody hell,' she snapped, whipping Ashley straight from his desirous daydreams of her. 'The bloody idiot didn't refuel. Why didn't I notice that before?' She pointed to the fuel quantity indicator. 'What sort of operation is Tom running here?'

'I don't imagine Tom knows.'

Jade hit the primer to inject some fuel into the engine, but it faltered. 'Idiot!'

The engineer popped his head into the cockpit, and said 'Miss, you're good to go. It was a faulty light, and nothing more.'

'Thanks,' she said, muttering about the incompetent pilot who'd last flown the Cessna.

They refuelled, and then idled at the end of the runway as she surveyed her control panel, triple checking everything before her.

'Jade, don't be so nervous. Everything is fine now.'

'I know it looks fine, but I am so tired. I don't trust myself.'

'Do you want me to fly?'

'No!'

'Jade, it's better to be safe than sorry. Don't consider relinquishing this flight as a sign of incompetence or failure. Just blame it on me lusting after you all night long,' he said, gently holding her hand.

'Are you going to be doing the same things again to me tonight, Mr Lyndhurst?' she asked, breathlessly trying to focus on the panel again.

'Would you like me to?'

Right back in her court. Why did he keep doing

71

that? Why was it always about what *she* wanted? What did he want? What did he feel towards her?

After refuelling, Jade repeated her registration number to Air Traffic Control, and prepared to motor for takeoff. But first, one more studied search of the control panel. She couldn't take off unless she felt one-hundred-percent confident in the plane, and herself.

As the wheels finally left the tarmac, Jade took note of the vertical speed indicator and ensured the transponder was registering to the guys on the ground.

'Perfect. That was a perfect take off, Jade,' Ashley smiled.

They made smalltalk for the duration, and Jade was surprised by how quickly the next hour whizzed by. Jade shared how she had plans for working at Roo Airlines for two years, and then talked about setting up a flying school for teenage pilots.

'That's what you really want to do? Train young adults to fly? I had no idea you were so ambitious. I'm sorry, Jade. If there's anything I can do…'

'Yes, don't force me to go back as your PA.'

'Which means not coming back as my wife,' he sighed. They were back to this crossroads again.

'I don't want to put my life on hold anymore.'

'Is that what you've been doing? Has your life been on hold all these years?'

What she wanted to say was that she wasn't going to wait around for him to notice her any more. Sure, he was noticing her now, but that was only to get her to come back to her old job, and to settle the alfalfa debt! Why couldn't he just see her as a desirable woman? Damn it, she wasn't ugly. She wasn't annoying (for the most part). They got on well with each other. What was the problem? And, furthermore, he was actually physically attracted to her. The sexual chemistry was explosive. But for some reason, this wasn't enough.

They were preparing to land when a ruckus came from the seating area.

'Something's not right back there.' Jade said nervously. When she put a call in over the intercom to her on-flight stewardess, there was no answer.

'I'll check!' Ashley said, knowing he should have been strapped in and not wandering about the aircraft.

Hennit was drunk, and had the stewardess cornered. With his lecherous hands feeling her up, the stewardess was crying. 'Leave me alone. Get back to your seat,' she whimpered.

'Get the hell off her!' Ashley yelled, lunging into him with a swift thump to the chin. 'Get off her, and get the hell back in your seat and strapped up. That's an order. I don't care who the hell you are. You fly on one of these planes, then you're an ordinary person following ordinary rules.'

What Ashley didn't expect was for Hennit to launch back at him. Considering the man had several glasses of rum, his aim was good. Ashley lost his balance, and the stewardess screamed.

'Go to the cockpit, and sit with the captain,' Ashley ordered her. 'Go!'

Ashley wrestled Hennit into a seat, and buckled him in. 'Don't you ever call Lyndhurst Incorporated Airlines again. And I'll sure as hell make sure you never fly with Roo Airlines. You can find your own way back. There won't be a return flight for you.'

'Whatever!' The arrogant Hennit spat at Ashley. 'Just get me to the ground.'

Upon landing, Hennit was met by a police escort,

and Ashley pressed charges on behalf of Roo Airlines. Within minutes of giving his statement to police, he phoned Tom Bradley and explained everything.

'I can't imagine what would have happened if you weren't on that flight. We've never had anything like this happen before. I might have to rethink having a ladies-only crew.'

'I wouldn't go that far, Tom. Both women are more than capable. It was just bad luck that they ended up with this jerk. When do you need Jade back?'

'Her next flight is to The Rock day after next. If I'd known she wasn't doing this return flight, I'd have booked her for something else. You guys have a good time.'

'Tom, thanks.'

'I'm fine,' she said, removing her shaking hand from his. 'I just want a coffee and to go to bed.'

'Not a good combination. Caffeine and sleep?'

'I'm not in the mood for science. Let's get a taxi and get to a B&B.'

So, she was tired, feisty as ever, and she didn't want to hold his hand.

Ashley took their pilot bags in one hand, and said, 'Sit over there for a few minutes, Jade. I'll make the phone calls. Have some water.'

When he returned a few minutes later, Ashley asked 'Ready?'; then he wheeled their luggage on a trolley, and said 'Follow me.'

'Taxi rank is this way,' she said, walking in the opposite direction.

'Yes, but we're going this way. Come on.'

'What?'

Ashley led her to the VIP area, and the door of a

limousine was opened.

'Ashley?'

The driver took the luggage and placed it into the boot.

Ashley watched her body collapse against the chic tuxedo-leather seats, and knew that she felt safe behind the tinted windows. There were no Hennits of the world here, and when Ashley poured some sherry from the crystal decanter into glasses, he heard her breathe a sigh of relief.

Within minutes, the stress of the flight and Hennit's disruption eased away. They drove slowly past the sophistication and culture of Melbourne, and arrived at their accommodation.

'This isn't a B&B, Ashley. My income doesn't stretch to this.'

'Mine does. And besides, it does provide you with bed and breakfast, so don't resist this. This place is intimate. You'll like it.'

'The Cullen,' she said to herself.

They walked into the reception area, where the walls were adorned by art from the contemporary artist, Adam Cullen. Escorted to their room, Ashley soon closed the door behind them.

'I never want to have an experience like that again,' she said, holding back the tears. 'That idiot could have killed us all!'

'Yes, he could have. But he didn't,' Ashley assured Jade, wrapping his arms around her while she cried.

When she finally calmed down, she looked up into his eyes then ran her fingers over his bruised chin.

'Does it hurt?'

'Not much,' he smiled. 'A small price to pay.' How did they go from employer-employee to this?

They stood by the bedroom window, taking in the sweeping views of Port Phillip Bay and the Melbourne Central Business District skyline.

'I might head down to the gym while you sleep,' he said softly, drawing her out of her thoughts. 'Chapel Street is just a few minutes away. Maybe you'd like to go shopping later?'

'Don't leave me alone.'

'What's wrong?' he asked. 'You'll sleep well in this bed, and you can block out the natural light. When you're rested, then we can make the most of our time here.'

'Don't you want to... aren't you tired?' Jade tripped over her words.

'I can wait till tonight. I'm fine, really.'

But as soon as he saw her face fall, he knew what it was really about. She wanted him.

'You need to sleep, Jade. And if I stay here we both know that's not going to happen. It's best if I go to the gym.'

As he watched her remove each item of clothing, the gym became a distant idea. Ashley helped her out her underwear, and then pulled back the covers of the bed.

Swiftly dismissing his own clothing, he was right there with her.

'Sleep,' he ordered. 'First, you sleep.'

Ashley's arms were around her, keeping her safe, and within minutes she was sound asleep. If only sleep had come as quickly to him. It didn't. Everything about his life was hanging in the balance. Emilia had emailed to say he needed to return to London; Leonie was sending love emails, and Hannah....well, Hannah had to be 'redistributed' around the office. There was no way she could be his PA. And what of his PA? Jade Stirling, who set life to millions of alfalfa seeds and got a little creative with red ink and silver scissors; what the hell was he going to do with her?

If he was honest, there'd never been a time when he saw his life without her by his side. It might have been in her capacity as a PA, but she was not an ordinary assistant. He'd always known that. Right from day one, she was the one who made him smile. There were times when he tried to remember life before she began work at Lyndhurst Incorporated, and those days were but a hazy, distant memory: there, but not there. Life, ever since Jade arrived, was in Technicolor.

Ashley recalled her second day on the job. Several staff members were in the office kitchen having lunch. One of the guys was grilling a cheese sandwich when the grill caught on fire. Everyone panicked. Some of the women screamed. Not Jade. She went straight up to the cooker and turned it off at the wall, removed the offending sandwich, and used a towel to extinguish the flames. Ashley had never seen such an act of calmness. Then and there, he knew that she was perfect for the job. The entire office staff soon learnt that Jade Stirling would be the calm shelter in any storm.

Slowly extricating her from his arms, he headed into the next room to phone his London office. 'Emilia, it's Ashley Lyndhurst. What's going on?'

'Mr Lyndhurst, everything's under control. It would help to know when you're coming back though, as I have to reschedule some of your meetings.'

'I appreciate that, but what was your message about? You said I had to come back urgently.'

'I have no idea what you're....' and the penny dropped. *Jesus, Jade!* Oh was she going to pay for this!

Emilia knew exactly what had happened. 'So, you've found Jade then? Everything going well, I take it?'

'Why are you changing the subject? Is everything okay in the office? What was with the email?'

'I'm sorry, Mr Lyndhurst. I got confused. I shouldn't have used the word urgently. Just come back when you're ready. How is ...*Jade*?'

'Everything's okay? Really? I don't need to come back straight away?'

'Perfectly okay. Jade's not the only person capable of running a tight ship!' Her voice was on edge, and he wondered why she was getting cranky.

'How's Hannah fitting in?'

'All thing's considered, she's doing well.'

'And the new filing system?'

'Sorry?'

'Her new chronological filing system? She emailed about changing my filing system and removing all the plants from the office.'

There was a silence at the end of the line.

'Emilia?'

'Mr Lyndhurst, you really shouldn't give too much thought to the office.'

'Have...ahem, has Leonie said anything to you about the recent business trip?'

'Leonie? Leonie's on annual leave. Don't you remember? She hasn't been here since...'

'Okay,' he said, interrupting her. 'Just let me know if there is anything urgent. In fact, Emilia, send it from your personal email.'

'Has Jade got one over you, Mr Lyndhurst?' she giggled.

'I'm afraid so,' he laughed in reply, trying to see the funny side. 'Yes, she most certainly has.'

'The good news is that the carpet in your home has been removed, and is being replaced today. It's good for you to return to as soon as you're back in London.'

'Well, that's a relief! Thanks for looking after things Emilia. It's good to be able to rely on you.'

'You're welcome, sir.'

On one hand, Ashley wanted to laugh at the idea of Jade writing those emails, but on the other he was angry. If she liked him so much why was she trying to get him to return to London so quickly? It didn't make sense! He paced the room trying to figure her out. Did she love him? Did she want to be with him? If so, why was she trying to send him away? Women! He'd never been able to fully understand them, and just when he thought he'd finally started figuring them out—or more accurately, figuring Jade out—all the rules seemed to have changed. What was he supposed to do? Did she really want him to leave? And why?

Ashley watched her sleeping, her breath rising and falling ever so gently; and he let her sleep, then stepped out of the room to make his next phone call.

'Tom, we have a situation. I don't want to go into the details, but Jade needs to move back to London with me. How much notice does she need to give you? Can I send a replacement pilot or two?'

'Mate, I know I owe you, big time, but you're putting me in a difficult position. I like Jade. She won't be happy about this.'

'Let me deal with Jade's moods. Just let me know what I can do to have her officially removed from Roo Airlines.'

'Let her do this last flight to Alice Springs, and then she's all yours.'

Ashley lay down in the bed next to her and felt Jade stirring beside him as he closed his eyes. It was time for him to sleep now. She could wait.

If he didn't know better, he was sure that he felt her eyes staring at him. What was she thinking? What was she plotting? Initially, he feigned sleep for about half an hour, and then slowly, slowly drifted off. Being horizontal for too long rendered him useless. When he fell asleep it was to the image of her in the lounge room that day, when the towel had just fallen to the ground; it was the first time he'd seen her naked, and the memory of her curvaceous hips, ample breasts, long legs, and slender shoulders brought a smile to his lips.

Jade watched him; her heart racing. This was the man she'd loved since she was eighteen years old. Almost every day since, she'd been by his side, pre-empting his every waking need. What on Earth was he doing in Australia? No one needed a PA that badly.

For years she'd imagined him making love to her, holding her in his strong arms, and now that it was a reality, she was confused. It still wasn't enough! She wanted *everything*. Yes, she wanted to be Mrs Lyndhurst, but she wanted more: she wanted him to love her with every single breath that he took. It was clear that it wasn't going to happen, and that she needed to move on. Marrying him to repay the alfalfa saga was not a viable way of having him. It was time for honesty. Jade knew that she could never be what he wanted, and it was time to focus on herself. Roo Airlines had been the first step in doing that, and now she had to plan her future. What did she want? Yes, she wanted to set up a flying school. It would be a place for after-school lessons, weekend lessons, and school-holiday lessons.

Jade pulled out her laptop and started writing a business plan. Five pages of notes later, she suddenly got the urge to check in on the Lyndhurst Incorporated emails.

Funny, why hadn't he replied to Hannah or Emilia? Then she logged into Leonie's account thinking he wouldn't have bothered with her email, either. But she was wrong.

Dear Leonie. What a fabulous time we had! Taking you away for two weeks was the best fun I could have had at work, if you know what I mean! And yes, I'd love you as my PA. When can you start? Combining business and pleasure is going to take on a whole new meaning if you know what I mean. Keep sexting me, it turns me on like you wouldn't believe. I'll be back in London in a couple of days. Thanks so much for letting me stay in your apartment. Who knows, maybe I won't go back to my penthouse? Yours, Ash.

Jade gasped. 'Oh My God,' she said. 'So he does like her?' Try as she might, she couldn't hold back the tears. Leonie and Ashley? Jade sobbed and sobbed, until she felt so wrung out that she could hardly stand. Soon the sadness and dejection gave way to anger. How dare he make love to her, how dare he make her feel special, when he had no feelings for her other than to make her pay for trashing his home? How dare he! Leonie? She wanted to scream. Leonie was her worst nightmare, and now Ashley wanted to be with *her*? 'I thought I was indispensible!' she snapped out loud. 'I'll break her neck.'

A noise came from the bedroom, and Jade made her way to the bathroom before Ashley could see the state she was in.

Under the steam of the shower spray, she let the tears fall. *How dare he!* Jade berated herself for being so stupid; for believing, even for a second, that he might be interested in her. Of course he wasn't! He was just a man. An ordinary man, simply meeting basic, biological needs, while attempting to re-employ his reliable PA. Jade wanted to scream at her own stupidity.

When his hands came behind her, carefully sitting around her waist, her words were simple: 'Get your hands off me, and never touch me again.'

Jade didn't look around at him, or say anything else.

Ashley removed his hands, but stayed under the shower, grabbed the soap and began washing himself.

The last time they'd spoken she was tired, vulnerable, grateful and desirous for him. And *now*? Now she wanted nothing to do with him. What the hell was going on? And then he realised: she'd read the email. Good! Truth-serum time.

'If you want to pull out of our merger, that's fine. I'll catch the next plane home. We can sever all ties. I can see you're ambitious, Jade. I don't want to get in the way of that. For some reason, I thought you liked me. I thought you loved me, but this was never about love; just lust and greed. This was only ever about you furthering your own ambitions. You played your cards so well, Jade Stirling. I thought…we might have been able to put our working relationship to mutual benefit. I was wrong.'

Jade spun around, her wet hair clinging to her scalp; her face desperate. 'Don't talk to me about ambition! You're so ambitious you can't even see what's under your nose. And anyway, I have every right to have my own dreams.'

'You want out, you can have out. But first,' and he swooped down over those damp lips and took her as if his life depended on it. Ashley was so hungry for her, he'd have done anything in the world for Jade; and the thought of walking away from her was insane. Jade was his world and always had been. Ashley knew that now; he just didn't know how to tell her. And he didn't know whether or not to trust his feelings. What if it was just a healthy dose of lust? It was important he didn't confuse his physical needs and desires with the heavy commitments expected of emotional attachments. The last thing he wanted to do was to break her heart; she deserved better than that. He had to tread carefully in this terrain.

As the warm water cascaded over their bare bodies, he became increasingly aware that she wasn't resisting him. Despite her earlier protestation about him never touching her again, she was drowning in the sensations. Ashley could have her right here, right now, in the shower, if he wanted. And he wanted her desperately. But first, he had a plan or two of his own.

Without warning, he abruptly let her go. 'I apologise. I'm sorry. You said not to ever touch you again, and I violated your wish. I'll leave now. Goodbye Jade.'

'Ashley. Ash,' she said, catching her breath. 'No. No. Don't go.'

Ashley turned back around and looked at her: she was flushed, wet, full of desire. Arousal was written all over her.

'I'm confused. Tell me what you want, Jade. And by God, make it quick because otherwise I'm going to take you right now!'

Would she admit to him that she wrote the emails? Did she think he'd find it as unforgiveable as a houseful of alfalfa sprouts?

'Leonie. I need to know about you and Leonie.'

She was jealous.

'Leonie Allan? From Human Resources? The same Leonie you're desperate for me to fire? What about Leonie?'

'Are you…' she turned away. Even the words felt torturous. 'Are you sleeping with her?'

'Are, as in present tense? I'm sleeping with you right now, Jade. Or, at least, I have been.'

'Have you had sex with her? Are you planning to go back and…'

'Jade, you've moved to Australia and have various ambitious plans before you, what difference does it make if I have or haven't had sex with Leonie? What does it matter to you if I go back and do to her what I've been doing to you this past week?'

Should he tell her that there was no way perfume-pot, gum-chewing Leonie Allan would end up in his bed? Ever!

'It matters.' Once again she turned away.

'How does it matter? You can't have everything your own way! If you only want me to be with you, then you have to meet me half way here. You can't expect me to stay sexually monastic while you're on the other side of the world building your dreams. If you don't want me to touch her, or any other woman for that matter, then what are you prepared to do to ensure that you're the only woman I have thoughts about?'

'Leonie's all wrong for you!'

'That's your only line of defence? Seriously? Jade, come on. You can do better than that. Why shouldn't I be with Leonie?'

'Because you should be with me!' she yelled, the anger astounding them both.

Ashley took a few deep breaths while deciding how to play this. He certainly didn't want to hurt her, but one thing was clear: she had to know that they were equals, and that for their relationship to work it had to be based on trust. 'Leonie loves me,' he said firmly.

'What?' Her eyes were flicking back and forth. 'What...What did you do on your trip away?'

'That's none of your business, Jade. Look, I offered you a marriage deal. Do you want it or not? This is my final offer.'

'I don't want a marriage deal! I want.... I want you! Are you so blind that you can't see I'm in love with you?'

'You love me? Prove it.'

'Prove it?'

'Prove you love me.'

'How?'

'I can think of a few ways...' he laughed.

'And do what you've been doing with Leonie? I don't think so!'

Jeez, Jade. What do you take me for? I've never had sex with her, and never will, for as long as I live! For God's sake, give me some credit!'

'But...'

'But what?'

'But you said she loves you, and that...'

'I know the emails were from you, Jade. I wanted to give you a taste of your own medicine.'

All at once he wanted to laugh at the millions of thoughts racing across her face.

'Oh,' was all she said.

'I don't fancy her in any way, or any other woman in that office. You have my word on that, but if you ever try a stunt like that again, I won't let you off so lightly.'

This time, when he kissed her, it was with the promise that she was the only woman in his life.

Ashley didn't bother drying either of them off with a towel. Instead, he scooped Jade up in his strong arms and carried her to their bed. Their bodies dripped water onto the silk sheets.

When his kisses continued to undo her, she moaned with each press of his lips against her damp skin; his hands moved tenderly from her head to her neck. His kisses soon followed, and at the nape of her neck he paused. Ashley breathed in the warmth of her smooth skin, closing his eyes as he did so.

'You're a complicated woman, Jade Stirling.'

'I'm not,' she moaned. 'I promise you I'm not. My needs are simple.'

He knew exactly what she wanted, so he lingered a little longer at her neck, returning to her ear lobes and nibbling the soft downy area.

Although her body pulsed with need, as did his, he refrained from rushing. His fingers brushed lightly over her shoulder, and then down the length of her arm.

Ashley's kisses moved to her navel, and he tenderly nipped at her belly.

Her body sighed with deep pleasure, and rose to meet him. It wouldn't be long until she demanded that he entered her. But she could dictate to him all she liked, Ashley thought to himself. *I'll take her when I'm damn ready, and not a second before.*

The pain of anticipation was unbearable. The build up of pressure in between her legs demanded to be released; she felt her hand slide there, encouraging him to follow, to be guided by her instructions. But still, he focused entirely on other parts of her body.

'Ashley...'

'Shhh. I'll get there when I'm ready,' he whispered.

'I'm ready now. Ash, I need you now.' Her breath was heavy, desperate and pained.

'I don't want to rush this.' He tried not to laugh when yet another moan escaped her damp lips. His hand met hers at the portal of pleasure, and he pushed her fingers out of the way as if to say 'my turn.' She seeped like dew on a flower, and he was like a bumble bee desperate to go inside. He paused at the precipice of pleasure; the pulsations tore through them. There was only one way to silence that noise. Only one way. Jade's body bucked with a need so great it almost hurt to be alive.

'Ash,' she moaned.

'Shhhh,' he replied watching the ecstasy tear through her body, from one end to the other. He looked up at her pleading eyes. Just another minute, he thought to himself. The truth was, he couldn't wait much longer either. He was so damn-near ready to explode.

Pleasuring her was excruciatingly arousing, but he needed to meet his own needs as well, and right now he needed to...

The gentle rhythm he'd maintained soon became urgent, their needs encouraging each other higher up the mountain of pleasure. They fitted together so perfectly, already knowing what each other's preferences were. So close, so close and yet so far. Ashley slowed right down, until every movement was slow, and then removed himself just before she peaked.

'Oh my God, Ash. What are you doing? Don't leave me like this. Not again.'

'I'm not leaving you anywhere.' He chuckled, and then lay on his back. 'I want you on top of me so I can watch you. Nothing gives me more pleasure than watching your face change expression.'

Couldn't he have said that earlier? Jade hoisted herself up onto an elbow and looked at him. 'That was cruel. Very cruel. Now I'll have to start all over again!' she said, straddling him. Within seconds, she was circling the mountain top, calling out as they detonated at the same time, manoeuvring themselves to be as close to each other's centre of pleasure as possible.

If he died now, his epitaph would read 'One contented man.'

Jade threw her head back as her body relieved itself of the torment, and then collapsed, sated, down against Ashley's strong chest.

'Let me take you out to dinner, Jade,' he said, half an hour later.

They showered, made love again, showered again, and then dressed.

A limousine drove them to a restaurant in the foothills of the Grampians. The Royal Mail was renowned for its outstanding menu. The waitress spoke eloquently about the 150 varieties of organic and heirloom vegetables, leaves and herbs produced by the restaurant's kitchen gardens each year.

'We also have orchards and an olive grove which provide stone fruit, apples, pears, berries, figs, quince and olives.'

Jade read through the menu: "Produce is also collected from the wild, and sourced from local artisan producers." For most of the evening, conversation was light and friendly. They seemed to have reached a silent compromise about the day's events.

Jade scrunched her linen napkin onto the plate. The pine nut, nettle, flaxseed winter truffle, parsnip and triple cream accompanied by charred young garlic, cauliflower and aged pecorino were exquisite.

Ashley had chosen eggplant in white miso, dried grains and cured kelp.

For dessert, Jade became besotted with the pistachio and hazelnut-honeycomb chocolate and they shared it, feeding each other off the one spoon. She felt her pulse race. Would she ever have enough of this man? Everything about him made her swoon. Her tongue traced her bottom lip, slowly, and she became acutely aware of the hunger in Ashley's eyes. Their hotel room seemed a long way from here.

'Two years, Jade. Just two years as Mrs Lyndhurst and then you're free to get on with your dreams. I'll even help you to achieve them. That's the least I can do for you for all your years by my side.'

Ashley described the eight new planes he wanted to add to his fleet, and the impending celebrity tour his company was flying. 'I really could do with your help for that.'

'Okay.'

'Okay to what?'

'Both. I'll marry you, and I'll help finalise the Serafina Simmo Tour. It's my speciality, so I may as well. Almost all the work is done for the tour anyway. There are just a few loose ends to tidy up.'

'I'll be a good husband to you, Jade. I promise.'

Jade was touched by the genuine look in his eyes, and the sincerity in his words, and smiled at him weakly. For the first time, she felt he deserved so much more than her.

'I can't promise I'll be a great wife. My track record with you hasn't been great, lately, has it?'

'True, but it hasn't put me off. I'm still here. Still game to try.'

Their eyes locked, both desperately searching the other and wondering what the future would bring.

Course Correction

Seated in the cockpit of a Cessna, Jade signalled to air traffic control that she was ready.

Takeoff was uneventful, and they settled into quiet conversation and sipped coffee. They were taking a team of movie executives to Ayres Rock for scouting. The location needed to be assessed for lighting, viability, weather, sound and so on. The team of seven were being catered for by two stewardesses. After her last flight, Jade was feeling a tad nervous about passengers. Ashley tried to reassure her that her previous flight was a one-off, and that everything would be fine.

'You've got a real talent for writing, and your office newsletters are always well received. How would you feel about creating an online magazine for our fleet?'

'Because you don't think I have enough work to do as your PA?'

'No, because I think you're brilliant at everything you do.'

'How long have you been planning this?'

'Just since this morning!'

'Well thought out, then?'

Ashley reached over and touched her hand. God she was gorgeous. Why hadn't this been more straightforward? Why hadn't he asked her out years ago? What an idiot!

'I've been such a fool, Jade. You've been right in front of me for years, and all I could think was that I couldn't break my own company's rules. I thought I'd be setting a bad example if I started dating one of my employees!'

'So what do you think will happen if you marry one? What sort of example will that set?'

'Well, you'll be more than my wife. You'll be my business partner.'

'What do you mean?'

'Lyndhurst will be half yours.'

'I hope you're joking?' she almost choked on her coffee.

'But why would you do something so stupid when this arrangement is only for two years? You haven't thought this through, Ashley!'

'I've actually given a lot of thought to this.'

'But if I leave…if I leave after two years then I'm legally entitled to take half of the business. That's nuts!'

'Is it? You've worked damned hard from the day you joined and many of those contracts happened because of you and you alone. I'm a fool in some ways, Jade, but not in others. I know exactly what you're worth.'

'I'll sign a pre-nup. The whole point of this marriage was to erase a few alfalfa plants into non-existence, not for me to whisk away everything you've worked for.'

'You still think there were only a few alfalfa plants, don't you?' he laughed in disbelief.

They flew into Connellan Airport at Ayers Rock.

As they walked into the resort hotel, Jade said 'Can you take my bag up to the room? I've got something I need to do.'

'Sure. Is everything okay?'

'Yep!' she smiled brightly, but something didn't seem quite right. Ashley watched her walk away, and his eyes never left her as she headed down the busy corridor. He watched from a distance as she stopped to speak to the woman at the Medical Services Area, then took a seat in the waiting area.

Was she sick? he wondered, then left to check into their room. Half an hour later she arrived there, avoided eye contact, and headed into the shower.

Within seconds he was there, holding her close. 'What's wrong? Are you sick?'

'No, not at all. I feel fine.'

'But you were at the Medical Services.'

'If you must know, I was getting a prescription for the contraceptive pill.'

'Why?'

'*Why?* Are you serious? Why?' she asked again in disbelief. 'Because I don't want to bring a baby into a marriage that's nothing more than a business arrangement. If I ever have children, I want them to be loved and wanted by both parents. That's why.'

Ashley held his hands either side of her face, and kissed her softly on the lips. Her almond-shaped eyes glistened, and her high cheekbones were gently rouged by the nature of their conversation.

It never occurred to him that she wasn't on contraception.

'And what makes you so sure I wouldn't want to have a child with you?'

'And two years later I take it away from you?'

'*If* you left in two years…'

Jade lowered her eyes to avoid his gaze.

'Look at me, Jade' he pleaded, pain etching into the baseline of his voice.

'Do you want children?'

'Yes.'

'Would you like children with me?'

'Why are you doing this to me? Why do you always do this? Why do you always put everything on *my* shoulders? Don't you have an opinion on anything? Why don't you ever tell me what you want, or what you feel…or don't feel, as the case may be?'

As he drew her in close, so there was no space between their bodies, his body language was a more than adequate indicator of what he wanted, and of whom he wanted.

'Jade, don't take the Pill. Besides, surely you know that those synthetic hormones won't do your body any favours.'

'And nor will having a child with a man who won't be part of my life in the future. I'll take the risk, thanks.'

'A child would always bind us together, Jade, no matter what choices you make. Our lives would be forever linked.'

'Do you want that? Do you want to be "bound to me forever", Ashley?'

'I can see no hardship in that, Jade. I'm used to you. Your company is easy, you're funny, usually, and you know me better than anyone else. We make a good team.'

'But do you want that?'

'Yes, Jade. I do want to be bound to you. Why don't we have a child together?'

'Are you serious?'

'Very.'

'But I wouldn't be able to work for you. There's no way I'd leave my child in daycare.'

'There's plenty you could do from home, even with a baby around. If you wanted to, that is. You could have your own PA, and run…'

'Stop. You're getting way ahead of us here. Having a baby is a serious responsibility. This isn't going to work. Ashley, a child deserves parents who love each other. It's tough enough having a child; doing it this way is all wrong.'

Ashley wasn't going to argue with her. No, not at all. His body did the talking, and she was right there with him. He turned off the tap, and reached for a towel. Quickly rubbing himself down, he scooped her up and carried her to their bed.

'You want me to love you, Jade Stirling, and for some reason you don't believe that's possible. If that's the only thing that's stopping you marrying me or stopping us having a child, then you need to know that I find you very loveable.'

'That's not the same as loving someone, though, is it?' Jade put him on the spot. Why was it so hard to say what he felt in his heart?

'Don't be pedantic, Jade.'

'Why do you always call me pedantic when you're losing an argument?' she said, frowning. 'You always do that!'

Ashley laughed out loud, and had to admit she was right. Damn it! 'But you *are* pedantic!'

'Define pedantic,' she laughed.

They watched the Sun set behind Uluru, and that night they dined at the award-winning Sounds of Silence barbeque buffet, under the stars. There was something about being in the middle of nowhere that acted as an invisible blanket, protecting them from the world. Though neither of them said a word, they both found themselves wanting to stay in this bubble for a long time.

Jade said her goodbye to Tom and the office staff at Roo Airlines, still in disbelief that he was so willing to let her go without notice. What hold did Ashley have over him? That thought occupied her throughout the flight back to England.

A Wedding to Plan

Everyone in the London office fawned over Jade when she returned. Their initial joy turned to deflation when they realised that only two people won the bet: most of the office gambled large sums of money that Ashley Lyndhurst couldn't woo Jade back to be his PA.

Ashley called a meeting, and the entire staff met at 5pm in the conference room.

'I know you're all tired and want to go home. I doubt any of you, however, are as tired as I am. Those long-haul flights are a killer. You'd think I'd be used to it by now. I've heard about the office bet. Shame on you guys! A little more faith next time, okay? Not only have I brought Jade Stirling back here to be my PA, we're getting married.'

Gasps, sighs from love-struck office juniors, and celebratory cheers went up in the air.

Jade smiled, but her tummy jangled into the future. It was all very well feeling happy now, but what would happen when her debt was paid? Nobody would be cheering then, or on the day she signed her divorce papers. Ashley Lyndhurst might have fancied her in his bed, and valued her as a PA, but one thing was perfectly clear: he *didn't* love her. Oh sure, she was loveable, but so was a Persian cat! If it was a cat he wanted, then he'd better prepare himself for the accompanying claws. One wrong turn on his part, and she'd do more than hiss at him!

'Right, Jade and I going to be tied up with the Serafino Simmo tour for the next few weeks, sorting out the fine details. Is everyone up to speed with their projects and flight schedules? Any questions?'

'Yeah, do we get wedding invitations?' yelled Sanjay from the engineering-administration department.

'I think we can arrange it,' Ashley smiled. 'Right, have a great weekend. See you all on Monday. 'Jade, can I have a word with you?'

His tone was stern. He'd never spoken to her in that capacity before, well, not in the workplace. Obviously things had been different—*everything* had been different—since the little alfalfa incident.

Once all the staff was out of earshot, he pulled her close.

'You need to access Leonie's email account and remove all traces of what you and I sent to each other, and ditto the ones from Hannah and Emilia.'

'Yes. I'll do it right away.'

As he saw the frown shadow her face, he realised his tone hadn't been friendly.

'I'm sorry. I was a bit on edge when I realised the whole office thought I had no chance with you!'

She laughed it off, and then said 'They weren't betting against you, they were betting *for* me. You see, they know me. They know that when I make up my mind about something, or *someone*...'

'Have you made your mind up about me, Jade?'

'Yes.' She changed the subject. 'Right, it's the weekend. I forbid you to do any work. Let's go home.'

'Home. That's an interesting word, isn't it? What have you done with your apartment?'

'Rented it out.' She paused, trying not to laugh. 'Got your carpets sorted out?'

'Apparently. Let's see, shall we?'

'On one condition.'

'What's that?'

98

'No shop talk this weekend. Let's just…let's just be Ashley and Jade.'

'I'd like that very much. Ashley and Jade.'

He reached for her hand, and lifted it up to his mouth. 'Ashley and Jade.'

Jade held her breath as the lift opened to the top floor of the building. The last time she'd been in Ashley's penthouse suite, her anger was out of control. Somehow, she could still see it all rather vividly: a violent scattering of tiny, kidney-shaped yellow-brown seeds strewn in anger across the beautiful carpet. A thick broom to hastily spread them out evenly and ensure they covered every square inch of the floors. Before turning on the fire sprinklers, she spent an hour cutting through his finest suits, and then hauling a year's worth of silk ties into a basin of ink. Three dozen containers of red ink. She remembered pouring every last one into the huge basin. 'Three times twelve equals thirty six,' she'd said to herself at the time.

As he opened the door, she reached for his hand and whispered 'I'm so sorry. I don't know what came over me. I really lost it.'

'Yes, you did. I know it hurt you that I took Leonie with me in your place, but try and remember just how ill you were. You are indispensible to me, but you're also human. I was trying to honour that. And your punishment just didn't fit the crime, Jade.'

Her skin flushed cerise, then veered sharply to claret. 'I know. I can see that. I really am sorry.' She searched his eyes, looking for answers. 'Will you… ever forgive me?'

'One day. Perhaps.'

When he pushed open the door, she could see

his relief: it was as if the jade-coloured alfalfa jungle had never been there. Thank heavens for Emilia's organisation skills.

Jade sighed with relief, too, and then Ashley pulled out his iPhone. After scrolling through a few pages, he then brought up some photos. 'Here, this is evidence of your crimes, Ms Stirling.'

'Wow, that's really…wow.' Jade's face lit up into a huge smile at her creative antics.

'Wow? Seriously? *Wow*? That's your idea of an apology?'

'But those little seeds were so…small. Well, you can't deny it was effective.'

'I'll show you effective,' he said, drawing her close and letting her body know how effective he could be. 'We've got a wedding to plan.'

'Not now. This weekend is meant to be free of work. You promised.'

'This weekend is about Ashley and Jade. And that's what this wedding is. It's personal. I'm hungry. Shall we order in or dine out?'

'That depends on how hungry you are Mr Lyndhurst,' she said, drawing her finger across his lower lip. 'Are you hungry?'

'Famished!' He carried her to the bedroom, and for a moment wondered if Emilia had the sense to get that room's carpet replaced as well. Relieved to see that everything was in order, he entered the room and threw back the covers on the bed.

'I think we should wait until our wedding night. That would be the right thing to do. And besides, surely my debt repayment plan doesn't start till I've said "I do", or am I wrong?' Jade asked.

'No chance! Consider this repayment of interest.'

'And are you interested in me, Ashley? Really interested?'

Ashley stopped, and looked at her. 'More than you could ever know.'

'Then tell me. Tell me what you're thinking. Tell me what you're feeling.'

'Actions speak louder than words, don't they?' he said, not giving her a chance to answer.

'I don't see what the problem is with getting married in a registry office. There's just no point doing anything fancy if it's not the real thing.'

'No, I want you to plan the wedding of your dreams,' he insisted. 'I'm having a shower, and then we should go out and have a bite to eat.' All this talk of registry offices dampened his mood for sex. It would have to wait.

As soon as she heard the shower fan switch go on, she searched through the contacts list on her phone and dialled Ashley's sister, Katrina. They'd hit it off years ago, and kept in regular contact.

'Kat, hi. It's Jade. I need a favour.'

'Sure. Anything.'

'I, er…as you know, I have a wedding to plan. I thought I knew everything there was to know about Ash, but this has me stumped. I have no idea of what he'd like in a wedding.'

'Ever thought of just asking him,' she laughed.

'It's not that simple. Kat, he still hasn't actually said he loves me. It's stupid. I'm sure he does. It's in every touch, and the way he looks at me, but trying to get those words off his tongue is like trying to launch a Concorde with water in the engine. It's just not going to

101

happen, and without those words it feels like something huge is missing. Tell me I'm overreacting.'

'Oh Jade. This isn't about *you*.'

'Of course it's about me!'

'There was life before Jade Stirling entered Ashley's world. And that life was called Angela Nightingale. It's not really my place to tell you this, but he was about to propose to Angela. He even got as far as getting down on one knee. Without even a strong drink behind him for Dutch courage, he told her he loved her and before he said another word...'

'What? What happened?'

'She laughed in his face. Something like "Love? Don't be so ridiculous, Ashley. Nobody marries for love!" Needless to say the relationship stopped dead in its tracks. Ash has never told me this. He's terribly private when it comes to affairs of the heart. I heard it from Angela's best friend who used to work at Lyndhurst Incorporated before you started there.'

'But why was she with him if she didn't love him?'

'Funny story that. I often wonder that myself. He even forgave Angela for her indiscretion.'

'What indiscretion? Kat? What?'

'Angela and Tom were at it like rabbits the whole time. Ashley caught them in bed together. It was about two years before he met you.'

'Tom? Not Tom *Bradley* by any chance?'

'Yeah, cousin Tom.'

'Tom is your cousin?' Jade sat down, her head reeling. 'Oh Kat. I can't believe he's never told me any of this before. He's never going to say he loves me, is he?'

'Never say never, Jade.' There was silence for a few moments, and then she continued.

'Oh, I don't know if I should mention this: Angela is now married. She goes by the name of Renry.'

'So?'

'Angela Renry is a wedding planner to the stars.'

'As if I'd use her to plan my wedding!'

Katrina laughed. 'No sillier than...never mind.'

'You think I should?'

'Just sayin' that "the wound reveals the cure" and all that.'

There was silence for a few moments while Jade processed the new information.

'How's your mum bearing up? Is she feeling any better?' Jade asked.

'Mum's still poorly. We get the test results tomorrow.'

'Good luck. Give her a huge hug from me. Seems like ages since Ash and I were up at the farm. Oh, Kat. Gotta go, Ash is out of the shower. Bye!'

Jade's mind started ticking over. That Angela woman certainly wouldn't be arranging her wedding, but curiosity was having its seductive way with Jade's thoughts.

The Wound

The Serafina Simmo world tour was about to begin, and although Ashley and Jade didn't need to accompany her or the Lyndhurst pilots, they agreed to meet up with her at various points to check everything was to her satisfaction. For Ashley, it was one of the biggest contracts of the past decade. Everything needed to run like clockwork. This contract, if it went well, would generate many more international superstars their way. In turn, he'd be able to employ more pilots and administrative staff. And, in time, he'd be able to cut back on his hours in the office and delegate some of his workload. He thought about how he'd spend his spare time, and every image he had of the future included Jade. Well, of course it did, he told himself. Jade was always going to be his PA.

Two large planes were required to accommodate Serafina and her crew of dancers, musicians, stage hands, instruments, sound systems, in-house media team, and various assistants. Serafina was performing in seventy cities, and fifty regional venues. Ashley knew that the vast majority of legwork for refining the itinerary and pilots' timetables was down to Jade.

'You've done an incredible job in organising this,' Ashley said to her. 'The thought of you not being back in London working on this fills me with dread. Thank you for coming back when you did.'

Jade looked him firmly in the eye. 'I didn't have a choice, did I?'

'You always have a choice. Are you saying you don't want to be here?'

'What I'm saying is that you didn't give me a choice.'

'You can walk away, Jade. If that's what you'd prefer, then I won't hold you to ransom. I'm not going to force you to stay with me.'

'So, you'd forgive and forget that little collection of seeds, then?'

'I will never forget what you did to my home and clothing, Jade. Never.'

Ashley looked down at his drink, and then said, 'I'll never forget you, either.'

They were in Boston, at the Ritz Carlton, to meet Serafina for lunch before her first US performance. 'Of course you had a choice, Jade.' Then he changed the subject. 'Everything is seamless when you're in charge of timetables and making sure the right people are in the right place at the right time. You've got a real gift for seeing the big picture and zooming down to the finest detail.'

The waiter took their request for drinks, and left them to wait for Serafina before ordering their lunch.

'Tell me about Tom Bradley. How are you connected? Why did he owe you? Why did he let me go without any fuss? Don't hide anything from me Ashley. If I'm going to be your wife, and not just your PA, I want the truth.'

'So, you're going to stay?' Ashley smiled in a self-satisfied way that made Jade want to slap him. 'Tom? Tom's my cousin. Our fathers were brothers.'

'But you have different surnames.'

'He uses his mother's maiden name. Long story, really.'

'Why does he "owe" you?'

Ashley looked at her for some time, wondering how much to reveal. It took him a few moments to construct his thoughts. Jade was going to be his wife, in every sense of the word. This wasn't a time for withholding information. But she really didn't need to know about Angela Nightingale. That woman was from his past, and he firmly intended to leave her there. They'd not had contact since their last day together; he had no idea where she was living or what she was doing.

'Our plane went down in Guatemala. Tom shouldn't have been flying solo, so I climbed in with him. The man was high as a kite, and, as it turns out, was carrying a load of drugs. I had no idea until we were in the air. I thought we were there to fly over new terrain. Turns out his dad had been a drug runner for years, and Tom was simply helping the "family business" right along. I had no idea, and my father would certainly have been blind to any such operation. Our plane went down in bad weather. I...I thought we were dead. We shouldn't have got out of there alive, but somehow we did. Tom was unconscious. We'd gone off radar, and there was no radio signal. The whole situation was a nightmare. I had drugs to get rid of before I could do anything else, otherwise if we did survive we'd have been in jail for a long time. I had to find help for him. I also had to get him out of the pilot's seat.' Ashley stopped talking for a minute as he relived the experience. 'For four days I walked through that stinking hot jungle, bitten alive by mosquitoes, with barely enough water to survive. I was sure he'd be dead by the time I found help, but by some miracle he was alive. Though, frankly, I wished he'd been dead. I had to write a statement about the accident, and said I was the pilot.'

'You did that for him? Why? He shouldn't be allowed anywhere near planes!'

'It's not that straightforward, Jade.'

'How can you condone that sort of behaviour?'

'He's my cousin! Tom's always looked up to me. You know my dad died in a plane crash. Well, his dad was with mine when it happened. It's hard to explain, but it bonds us. We both understand the shock of losing your father in this way. And we both understand that the drive, the *need*, to fly is still there…even though we know the dangers. I overlooked the drugs because, at heart, he's a decent bloke. *Most* of the time…'

'But you don't fly. Well, not that often.'

'I do enough to keep up my hours. I love being in the air; that feeling of power during take off; the power of lifting that silver bird into the air. It's exhilarating. But I've come to love the business side more.'

When Ashley placed his hand over hers, it was all she could do not to pull away. *So, he's not going to tell me about Tom and Angela. Fine. Just fine!* Jade withheld her temper. *You want secrets, buddy, I'll give you secrets!*

'And you, Jade. What about you? All you want to do is fly?'

It was hard to be furious with him when he was speaking to her in such a gentle way. It was as if he really cared about her plans.

'After that experience with Hennit, something's changed. I love the responsibility of contracts and deadlines, and seeing projects and plans come together. I thrive on it, and of course, that feeling of a job well done. But the responsibility of someone's life in my hands? I don't think I'm cut out for it. I was terrified with his behaviour. I know he was drunk and not in control of his senses, but there are so many things I can't control when I'm up in the air. Not to mention that idiot pilot who hadn't refuelled. Tom Bradley is a nightmare!'

'Don't blame Tom for a lazy pilot's behaviour. You know that Lyndhurst pilots would never do that?'

'Yes, logically I know that...but every time I get into a cockpit I'm at the mercy of other people's practices.'

'And your plans for a flying school?'

'Honestly? I just don't know. Everything feels so up in the air.'

They both laughed at the pun.

'Let's do the Serafina Tour and the wedding, and then see what you feel like then.'

They continued making small talk for a while, then Jade looked up at him quite seriously.

'Are you happy, Ash? Are you satisfied? Do you have everything you want in life?'

'Does anyone? There's no end point where everything comes together, Jade. Life is always going to have its ups and down. You have to go with the flow and from time to time reappraise if it's still the direction your heart wants you to go in. It's not unlike a pilot's course correction.'

'Do you follow your heart, Ash?'

'Yes, I do.'

'Then why won't you let yourself fall in love with me? You say I'm easy to be with, and you're even prepared to have a child with me...'

'To *raise* a child with you.'

'Raise...but you don't value me enough to fall in love.'

'How do you know I don't?'

'Because, despite what your body tells me, you haven't once said you loved me. You say that I'm loveable. But that's not the same thing. We both know it.'

'They'd just be words. Actions are more meaningful.'

'Ashley, I need the words. I need to hear them.'

'Would it genuinely make you happy?'

'If you meant them, then yes it would.'

'Great place,' Serafina swooned, taking in the ambience of the Artisan Bistro. Tall, with jet-black hair as long as the length of her back, and eyes of forest green, she looked like a mythical goddess. Today she was dressed simply in faded jeans and white t-shirt, a far cry from her on-stage persona.

Ashley ordered a generous plate of appetisers to share: truffle fries in roasted garlic aioli.

'Why have you chosen to start your tour with Boston?' Jade asked.

'It's my birth town. It seemed the logical choice,' the singer replied.

Serafina chose barbequed chicken with pineapple for her lunch, while Jade opted for vegetable pitta: zucchini, eggplant, roast peppers, quinoa and salad. Ashley chose the mushroom and caramelised onion burger.

'I didn't think there'd be anywhere we could have a quick bite to eat that was this tasteful. Well done Ashley,' Serafina said. 'And Jade, you've done such a marvellous job. I'm so used to organising everything myself. It's reassuring to be able to put this much trust in someone. Thank you.'

'It's my job,' Jade said modestly.

'No, this is so much more than a job. You're

passionate about excellence in customer service. It shines through everything you do. I hope he pays you well!' The women both laughed.

Ashley replied 'I am pretty sure I do.'

Finishing the last mouthful of his blueberry bread pudding, he looked at Jade and said 'She's priceless.'

Priceless isn't the same as "I love you", she said to herself. *Not the same at all, Ashley Lyndhurst!*

They went through the itinerary, and Serafina's needs, one more time.

'Everything is in place, and if by any chance there's a problem, we have pilots and contacts around the world who can step in at a moment's notice and support you or the piloting team until we can get there and take over. That's the beauty of being a worldwide firm. There really isn't anything to worry about. This is what we do, Serafina. You need to just focus on your concerts. That's what you do,' Jade said firmly but kindly.

Serafina pulled out two backstage passes. 'If you've got time, I hope you'll come and see the show tonight.'

Jade tried not to squeal, but Serafina could see the delight rushing through her body.

'We wouldn't miss it!'

'Oh, and here are passes to my other shows for the Lyndhurst pilots. Can you pass them on? So, we'll catch up in India next month?' Serafina asked, then picked up her handbag and gracefully left the building.

'Yes, we'll be there,' Jade called after her.

They spent the next few hours walking the upmarket shopping district before returning to the Ritz-Carlton

Club suite. It was luxurious, and for a hotel was incredibly comfortable, exclusive and intimate. Its reputation for attention to detail was well deserved, and Jade found herself enjoying the pampered experience of high living. Their master bedroom, with king-sized bed, featured city views. The large living room had French doors to a balcony. The state-of-the-art sound system filtered music throughout the luxurious suite. Jade and Ashley shared the large marble bath, splashing each other in bubbles and sipping champagne. 'Here's to us, Jade Stirling.'

'Here's to an amazing work life!' she countered as they sipped from each other's crystal glasses. 'It doesn't get much better than this, does it?'

Later, they dressed for the concert. Jade's dress was crushed silk and velvet in ecru, down to her calves; cinched in at the waist, with pleating to emphasis the bust. She let her dark hair hang loosely around her shoulders.

Ashley wore more relaxed attire: faded jeans and muslin long-sleeved shirt. It was a concert, after all. The cedar and spice aftershave he splashed on always left Jade weak at the knees.

As a result, she was now having second thoughts about leaving the hotel. Desirous for him, the thought of waiting several hours before she could remove his shirt was just too much for her. Life was never this complicated when she was just his PA. Back then, she could look at him longingly for several minutes at a time, with him none the wiser. Sometimes their hands would brush alongside each other as they exchanged documents. Jade would savour every second. At other times, she stood right next to him as he signed letters, breathing in that very same aftershave. But in those days, she could only imagine what it would be like to be in his arms. Now that she actually knew what it was like; the impact of that aftershave was deadly.

'Let's have a bite to eat at the Avery Bar before we head to the stadium,' he suggested.

It was classic 1950s, sleek and sophisticated, with warm colours, unusual light fittings, Italian marbled floors, and sisal rugs. The arch-shaped bar was dramatic, and boasted a chandelier which washed the place in warm lighting. They sat by the fireplace, engaged in their own world, sipping cocktails.

Between them, they shared bowls of marinated olives, eggplant caponata, marinated stone fruit, cucumber and avocado sushi, balsamic figs and crackers. As Ashley watched Jade licking her fingers, he drew close to her and whispered 'You know, Serafina wouldn't notice if we weren't there. That is, if you preferred to...'

'Ashley Lyndhurst! Of course we're going!' Jade laughed out loud, and pulled him towards the reception area of the hotel.

A concierge arranged for a limousine, and within minutes they were being escorted backstage to the Serafina Simmo *All Loved Up* Opening Concert.

Jade danced all night long, and Ashley, reluctant at first, was soon having the time of his life. Working life left little room, for either of them, for this sort of fun . As she danced, Jade's hair swung around her shoulders. Her cheeks were flushed, and she looked radiant.

Before Serafina's last song, she spoke. 'This song is dedicated to two love birds: Ashley and Jade. May you have a long and happy life together.'

Jade felt herself gulp, and cast her eyes away from Ashley.

Ashley lifted her chin up so that they could look into each other's eyes.

'I hope we have a long and happy life together too,' he said, trying to reassure her.

Yeah, but what about a *loving* life? She wondered. Would that ever happen?

In This Together

'You've been sick three mornings in a row, Jade. Your period is thirteen days late. Something you want to tell me?'

'How do you know?' she said, holding her hand over her mouth.

'Because every twenty nine days there's a large bar of dark chocolate on your desk, and if anyone goes near it you bite their head off. Haven't you ever noticed that I always tell you to go home an hour early on those days? I figured the chocolate was your monthly magnesium kick. There's been no chocolate this month.'

Suddenly, she turned her head and reached for the toilet again. Jade stood up, and washed her face.

'When were you going to tell me?' he asked.

'Are you okay about this? About us having a baby?'

'I couldn't be happier!' he said, smiling with delight.

'Really? Don't you feel...*trapped*?'

'Not in the slightest.'

Jade sank into his arms with relief.

'This is the best news I've had in ages. I'm thrilled Jade. We're having a baby. What's not to be happy about? Are you okay?'

'Shell shocked. I really didn't think something like this could happen so quickly.'

'You're young, fertile, healthy. Your body is probably throwing out eggs like raindrops.'

'Yeah, probably. But...'

'But what?'

'It changes everything. Having a baby is a huge thing. My life is never going to be the same again. Ever.'

'What are you worried about?'

'You. Us. The three of us. I don't want to…'

'You don't want what?'

'I don't want to leave you when my debt is paid. I want us to be a family. I want…damn it, Ashley. Why can't you tell me what I want to hear? I need to know that you're 100% in this.'

'I am. I assure you, I am. I want this as much as you do. I'm not going anywhere. I promise.'

Ashley passed her a towel so she could dry her face some more.

'Are you going to be up to the Industry Awards Dinner tonight? We don't have to go,' he said.

'Of course we're going. But I might need to spend a few hours on the sofa first!' Jade walked into the living room, and sank down into the maroon-covered lounge suite. Ashley came from the bedroom with a blanket and pillows. 'Let me know what you need. Anything at all.'

Ashley sat in a nearby armchair as if on sentry duty.

Jade could see the sincerity in his eyes; he'd do anything for her; anything, that is, except declare his love. Jade eventually fell asleep, and dozed fitfully through the afternoon.

By five o'clock, Ashley woke her with a gentle kiss. 'Honey, are you okay?' The concerned tone nearly caused her to weep.

'I'm fine. Is it nearly time to go?'

'When you get dressed it will be.' Ashley helped her out of the sofa, and led her to the bedroom.

Jade showered, and then chose something to wear. 'I really needed that sleep. Thank you. I feel so much better now.'

Ashley zipped up the back of Jade's turquoise, raw-silk dress, and then placed his arms around her, breathing in the warmth of her skin.

'You look gorgeous,' he whispered, their eyes catching each other's in the mirror before them. 'Are you sure you're up to coming out this evening?'

'I wouldn't miss this for the world.'

'I can't believe we're having a baby. This is so exciting!'

Jade wanted to share Ashley's joy but was too concerned about what the future held; she wanted their baby to be loved by their parents, but just as importantly, she wanted the baby's parents to love each other.

Lyndhurst Incorporated won the Airline Market Leadership award for five years running. It was becoming a standard joke in the industry that the competition must be rigged. Ashley most certainly wasn't planning to win it tonight; not for a sixth year. With Jade by his side, he felt he'd already won the greatest prize of all. Ashley also knew that the Market Leadership award was down in no small part to the tireless work Jade did on promoting his business. He wanted everyone to see that she was more than his PA. When he thought about it, he couldn't remember a time in his life when he felt more proud than he did right now, with her on his arm. And they were having a baby! It would be several weeks before they shared the news with anyone else, but right now he wanted to shout it to the world: *I'm going to be a father!*

The compère cleared his throat and said 'You might think that you know the answer to who has won our next award. It's a running joke, but I can honestly

tell you that I have no idea what is inside this envelope.'
He ripped open the gold envelope and smiled. 'The winner of this year's Airline Market Leadership goes to....Can anyone guess?' Laughter erupted throughout the audience before he continued: 'Lyndhurst Incorporated.'

Ashley stood up, and reached for Jade's hand. 'Come on, honey. This is yours, too.'

In a hushed whisper she said 'This is your award, not mine.'

Ashley's grip on her hand was firm. They made their way onto the podium to the applause of the good and the great of the aviation industry.

The auditorium was bathed in chandelier light, and journalists' cameras were flashing staccato style.

'This award is every bit as thrilling to receive as it was last year, and the year before, and...'

The audience laughed, and thunderous applause rumbled through the room.

'Many of you know who this award really belongs to: Jade Stirling. For years, so many of you have insisted that she must be more than just my PA; that she indeed runs Lyndhurst. You're right. Jade is so much more than what her CV indicates. I'm proud to say that Jade will soon be my wife.'

Media cameras went into overdrive, and there was a standing ovation. Jade's eyes brimmed with tears. Every set of eyes was upon her. Never in her life had she stood in the spotlight. For years she'd worked tirelessly behind the scenes. That was her comfort zone. Not this!

The walk back along the red carpet seemed to take ages. They returned to their seats with a maze of hands thrust in their path offering congratulations. No sooner were they sitting, than the compère announced a new award for the industry.

'Times are changing, and the aviation industry has been a leader in many advances. One such advance is the recognition of planes on environmental impact. This year, for the first time, we are presenting the Eco-aviation Award. This is open to all airline companies and businesses worldwide, and we hope this award will set a benchmark for everyone in this industry.'

The compère opened the final gold envelope, and said 'The inaugural Eco-Aviation Award goes to…' and he let out a chuckle. 'Lyndhurst Incorporated.'

Jade and Ashley looked at each other in shock. 'Did you know anything about this?' he asked her.

'Nothing. Honestly. I was asked to send in our environmental impact report, and our eco charter, but that's it. I promise.'

Again, he held her hand. 'Come on.'

'Ash…'

'We're in this together, remember?' The applause was deafening.

Ashley ushered her to the microphone.

'I want you to accept this award, honey.'

Jade blushed. Why did he always put her completely out of her comfort zone? No matter how often he did it, she never found it any easier.

'This award is a wonderful honour, but more than that, it feels incredibly personal. The environment is something close to my heart, and aviation has felt somewhat at odds with that. I hope that we can combine an ethos which supports the new innovations in flying as well as in nurturing the planet. Ashley and I are…' she looked up at him, then continued 'expecting our first child.' The applause barrelled through the room. 'I can only hope that as the years go by, this award truly becomes a symbol of our dedication to preserving the planet and honouring mankind's strident advances in technology. Children are the future, and this award is a constant reminder of each and every one of us to be mindful guardians of the planet. On behalf of Lyndhurst Incorporated, thank you.'

The entire staff of Lyndhurst was seated to the back end of the banquet area, and Jade could see the rumour mill in espresso mode.

'Guess we should have told them first,' she whispered as they sat back down.

'The announcement was perfect. Thank you. I couldn't have said it better myself.'

Jade fiddled with his bow tie. 'You look incredible, Ashley. Of all the awards I've been to with you, this is most definitely my favourite. I couldn't be happier.'

'Neither could I.' Ashley kissed her gently on the cheek, then suggested they mingle.

The evening was a success, socially and professionally. Ashley had built his business from the ground up, starting with just two small planes. In ten years, it had become an international success story which other aviation businesses modelled themselves on.

It was a little after two a.m. when they finally arrived home.

As Ashley helped Jade out of her gown, he kissed her bare shoulders. 'Did I tell you how ravishing you looked tonight?'

'No, you must have forgotten.' As they lay together, Jade said 'I love you Ashley Lyndhurst.'

After he kissed her on the lips, he replied 'And I am so very grateful for that.'

As Ashley held her, he was deep in thought. Jade valued honesty and loyalty. More than anything, he wanted to give that to her. Jade's love reminded him of dark chocolate truffle, with a hint of chilli. There was something dark and bittersweet about it. Their marriage was going to be both delicious and scary! It would keep him awake at night, and raise his blood pressure. Jade Stirling wasn't going to love him 'just a little bit'. No, she was going to be all consuming; a soulmate, in every sense of the word. And Jade deserved this love, this intensity, to be reciprocated.

For the first time, he couldn't help smiling about how jealous she'd been. Then he thought about his sin: taking Leonie on a business trip. One thing was for certain with Jade: innocent until proven guilty didn't apply. That wife of his was going to keep him on his toes for a very long time! It occurred to him that when it came to intimacy, Jade was fearless. If only he had the same trait. Then he'd be able to put her out of her misery.

A lesser man would have been unnerved by her complete attention and devotion to him, but Ashley had to admit that he found it flattering. As he watched her gently drifting off to sleep, Ashley silently vowed to be loyal to her. Truth was, he wanted to marry her now, but she'd already said that she had to wait till the morning sickness had abated.

Devil in Disguise

'Angelic Wedding Planning, Adele speaking. How may I help you?' the lyrical voice at the end of the line said, as if by rote.

'Hello, I was interested in booking a planner for my wedding.'

'We have five wedding planners here at Angelic. Did you want to request one in particular?'

'Does Angela Renry still work there?' Jade asked, suddenly wondering if this was a good idea. Trust Kat to put the idea into her head!

'Yes indeed. Would you like to make an obligation-free appointment?'

'Yes, thanks.'

'Mrs Renry has 12.45pm free on Thursday. Would that time work for you?'

'Yes. That's perfect. I can come in my lunch hour. Harley Street, right?'

'That's right. Thank you for your call.'

Thursday came around just a little too quickly, and Jade was having doubts. She'd promised Ash there'd be no more surprises. How was she going to explain this?

'I'm just popping out for a bit,' Jade said, not giving Ashley time to answer. 'I'll pick you up something to eat while I'm out.' She didn't look behind her to see that he could tell she was up to something.

'Jade?'

But she was out the door and pretended not to hear.

Angelic Wedding Planning was in a pure-white building, and the display window had no less that five virginal-looking brides head to toe in snow white.

'Aggghhh,' Jade muttered. The golden cherub figures were the only things that kept Jade from staying rooted to the pavement. They were rather endearing.

She immediately recognised the receptionist from her voice.

'Hi, I'm Jade. I have an appointment with Mrs Renry at 12.45.'

'I'll just call through and check if she's ready for you.' Within a few seconds, she looked up at Jade and said, 'Take the first door on the right. No need to knock.'

'Thank you.'

As she stepped into the office of Angela Renry, it was all she could do not to laugh out loud. It was wall-to-wall in fairy-floss pink, and she felt nauseas. It might be a little girl's dream, but a grown woman's? Jade held back the gag reflex.

One thing was clear: this woman would not be planning her wedding. But for now, just for now, she had a plan.

'Mrs Renry, so pleased to meet you. I'm Jade.'

'Jade. Tell me all about your dream wedding, and then I can tell you how we can work together.'

Despite the sickening hues of pink, there was something rather harsh about the woman that Jade just couldn't reconcile with the office, the building, and the nature of the business. And more than anything, she couldn't for the life of her imagine Ashley ever being interested in a woman like that.

What sort of hold did she have over him?

Why did her rejection of his love clamp down his heart so severely?

'My dream wedding is about one thing, Mrs Renry. It's about love. The love between my man and I. It's about that feeling when you know that you'd do anything for the other person. I want my wedding to show our friends and family just how much we mean to each other. What do you think of love, Mrs Renry?'

The saccharine smile which she'd worn suddenly evaporated, and her facial expression became glacial.

'My opinion isn't what's important here. This wedding is about your dreams and hopes.'

'Yes, but if I'm going to put the planning into your hands, then I need to know we're on the same page,' Jade said, smiling brightly, all the while wanting to hit the woman over the head with her handbag. How dare this hard-hearted woman break Ashley's heart. How dare she! Oh my god was she going to pay!

'Love is…well, it's personal. We all have our own ideas about what love is.'

I know your game, Renry, Jade muttered inside her head. *You'll pay for what you did to Ashley. Oh my how you'll pay!*

'Do you guarantee your work, Mrs Renry?'

'I'm sorry! What on Earth do you mean?'

'If your client isn't happy, do you offer a 100% refund?'

'I've never refunded a client in the entire time I've had this business.'

'That's not what I asked. If your client isn't happy…'

'Well, of course I would. Jade, I'm not sure how we can work together when we seem to be at odds…'

'I'm not at odds, Mrs Renry.'

Jade enjoyed saying the woman's married name.

Each time she did, it took Angela Nightingale further away from Ashley Lyndhurst.

'I just want to be clear that I'll get my needs met, and that if they aren't, you and I can both be honest about that. It's a simple practice of business.'

'Yes, of course it is. I'll get my secretary to draw up a contract offering a 100% refund if you're not happy.'

'Perfect.'

'Shall we get to work now on what you'd like? I've got another half hour till my next client.'

'Of course.' Jade's brain was working overtime. 'My fiancé, A…his name is Leigh. He's ever so busy, so our first few sessions will just be the two of us. I'd love you to meet him though.'

'It's essential that I meet Leigh. Wedding planning is based on the wishes of both people, not just one of them. What does Leigh do?'

'It's hard to explain, really. His work involves innovation, eco awareness. That sort of thing.'

There was no way she was going to even mention the aviation industry. That would be an instant giveaway.

'Here's a list of questions I give to every couple. If you fill this in, it will give me a good idea of the direction we're going in. Take it home with you, and if you and Leigh could fill it in then email it to me or send it back by post, then I can have a plan ready for our next meeting.'

'I'll do that. Shall we meet again next week?'

'Yes, we'll need to meet quite regularly if you want to have your wedding so soon.'

Jade had a skip in her step when she walked back to the office. One hundred-percent refund if the client isn't

124

happy. Suddenly she felt like an errant fifteen-year-old school girl who'd just defied her teacher. And it felt damn good!

'Honey, what did you bring me for lunch?' Ashley asked her when she came bounding into the reception area of Lyndhurst Incorporated. When she looked at him blankly, he asked her again.

'Ash, I...'

'What did *you* have for lunch then?' he asked.

'Nothing. I...I got sidetracked.'

'Is this what they call pregnancy brain?' he laughed. 'Come on, let's go out together and get a bite to eat. You can tell me what sidetracked you!' Ashley laughed and then winked at Emilia and Hannah on reception, as he escorted Jade out of the building.

'You look pretty pleased with yourself. What was it? A new dress?'

'I didn't buy anything. Not yet.'

They ducked into an upmarket Greek restaurant, and settled into their chairs. The waiter took their orders, and Jade shared that she'd just met with a wedding planner. They dined on a platter of vine leaves, olives, hommous, pitta and Greek salad.

'Did you make much progress?'

'Well, we really just go to know each other a little.'

'I'm not sure why you need a planner. I know that work's busy, but Jade, you're one of the most competent and organised people I know. Surely you can organise a wedding?'

'So competent that I forgot your lunch!' she laughed, trying to change the subject.

'What do you want in the wedding?' he asked, taking her hand in his.

'Simple. Close friends and family. No fuss. No white dress!'

Ashley laughed. 'I think the white would be a bit out of place with a pregnant bride.'

'Just a tad! And you? What do you want? And please, don't give me the line about weddings being a woman's thing. If you want to get married, then you have to tell me what you want. And besides, An... Angelic Wedding Planners has insisted that you declare your every last nuptial wish!'

'I want to stand beside you and promise to honour and respect you. I want to make vows of devotion and dedication.'

'And there we go again, Mr Lyndhurst. That L word just isn't going to show up, is it?'

'Damn it, Jade. You know what I feel about you. Why is this such an issue? Haven't I shown you in a hundred little ways how much I care for you?'

'Damn it, Ashley. You know what I feel about you. Why is this such an issue? Haven't I ...' she mocked him by repeating his words to him, but she was crying now. 'I need to hear you say you love me. I know you care for me. Why can't you say those three words: I love you? I mean, seriously, how bloody hard is it?'

'Jade, you don't understand.'

'I want to understand. Why don't you trust me? Why don't you help me to understand?'

Ashley signalled to the waiter for the bill.

'So, once again we're just going to leave this unresolved? Why are we even getting married?' she asked.

'Alfalfa sprouts.'

'Oh yes, of course. Stupid me. What an idiot to think you might have actually fallen in love with me by now. This is all about me paying you back! Some free and easy sex whenever you feel like it, that's all it's about, isn't it?' Jade stood up, furious with him, and walked back to the office, alone.

'Emilia, I'm not to be disturbed this afternoon. Not even by Ash. I need a few hours to work on something in peace and quiet.'

Emilia looked at Hannah, and when Jade shut her office door behind her, she whispered 'Do you think they just had a fight?'

Hannah mumbled, 'But I thought they were all loved up?'

'Ladies? Whispering?' came the baritone sounds of Ashley as he entered the foyer. 'Where's Jade?'

'Sir, she said she's not to be disturbed this afternoon.' He saw Hannah gulp, the lump in her throat jumping up and down in fear. 'Not even by you, sir.'

'Women!' he muttered as he strode into his office, slamming the door after him.

'Definitely a fight,' Hannah mumbled.

Jade spent the afternoon going through the wedding planner's questionnaire. There were two sets of 100 questions. A set for each person.

Jade found it frustrating that each question only had room for a one-sentence answer, so she started typing her responses and provided several paragraphs for many questions. She'd make Angela Renry pay. As she answered Ashley's questions on his behalf, she ensured that each response was diametrically opposed to hers.

'This is fun!' she said to herself, and her mood perked up quite a bit.

Jade stood up and put on the radio. She found her

hips moving seductively to Michael Bublé as he sang *Sway*.

Jade's favourite colours: white, pink.

That'll keep Mrs Renry happy, she thought to herself. Easy to work with something you're so familiar with!

Leigh's favourite colours: army green and tan brown.

Hmmm, try fitting those army-camouflage hues with your virginal white!

Jade's favourite music: Mozart
Leigh's favourite music: Heavy Metal.
Jade's preferred confetti: dried roses (pink!)
Leigh's preferred confetti: metallic

Jade's wedding song for the first dance:
Can I Have This Dance (for the rest of my life)?

Leigh's wedding song for the first dance:
I'll never fall in love again.

Jade's preferred flowers: scented pink roses
Leigh's preferred flowers: plastic black lilies

Religious or humanist wedding:
Jade, religious. Leigh, humanist.

Budget: Jade, unlimited. Leigh, £50,000

Jade's chosen décor: traditional and vintage
Leigh's chosen décor: modern and sleek

Church? Jade, yes. Leigh, no.

Hotel? Jade, no. Leigh, yes.

Number of guests. Jade 500, Leigh, 50

Who is giving the bride away? Giving herself away.
Writing own vows? Jade, yes. Leigh, no.

'Right, Mrs Renry,' Jade said out loud as she emailed the questionnaire to her. 'See how brilliant you are now!'

Within five minutes, Mrs Renry emailed her back.

To: Jade Stirling
Jade, we have a little problem here. I really don't think you and Leigh are very compatible. I wouldn't normally say this to a couple, as it's none of my business. I'm just concerned that... How long have you been together? How do you live with each

other when your tastes are so different? Don't get me wrong, I'm more than happy to work with you both, but we have to find the middle ground. I am going to need to meet with Leigh sooner rather than later.

To: Mrs Renry

We're so desperately in love with each other that our different tastes have no bearing. Honestly! I'm sure you can work your magic! You come highly recommended. And, after all, you're the one who knows all about love!

And the sex. Oh my. Let me tell you! It's just so hot! When he touches me, seriously, I just turn to butter. He knows all the right spots to hit. *Sigh* He takes me three times a day, you know, and then again at night. Can you believe it? As you could probably imagine, when you're this compatible in bed then the other little differences just don't matter, do they?

Jade had no sooner pinged off the email, when her office door opened.

'Why are you looking so pleased with yourself?' Ashley asked, walking over to her side of the desk.

'Nothing. Absolutely nothing,' she lied, closing down the lid of her laptop to hide all evidence of her latest adventure. 'Ready for home?'

'I don't know what you're up to Jade, but I hope it's legal.'

'Perfectly.' Jade dipped her head so he wouldn't see the huge smile on her face, but it didn't work.

'You *are* up to something! I knew it. Come on, what is it?'

'Nothing! Home. Now!' Again, she had to turn away from him because laughter was ready to erupt. For a few moments, she fussed at a nearby filing cabinet while she composed herself.

Jade had two more meetings with Angela before arranging for her to meet Leigh. 'We're just so in love. I couldn't be happier. I know you're just going to love him as much as I do,' Jade swooned. 'He's such a darling!'

Jade observed Angela trying not to gag at all her gushing.

There was nothing Angela hated more than sentimentality. There was one reason she was in this business, and one reason only: to make money. If she'd learnt anything from her old boyfriend, Ashley Lyndhurst, it was this: provide people with something they need, and then you'll earn the big bucks. Women were, for the most part, clueless, when it came to planning weddings, so it was easy for Angela to channel her energy into organising other people's lives when they were at their most vulnerable: madly in love.

'Can you meet Leigh this Friday?' Jade asked. 'Actually, do you know what would be really lovely? Why don't you come to our home to have lunch? We won't keep you for long, and then you can be back in the office in no time.'

'Sounds lovely,' Angela smiled feigning delight. Jade Stirling was really starting to irritate her. There had never been a client quite like her, and she was this close to cancelling their agreement. But it was a lot of money to just throw away because of a personality clash. Too much money, in fact, to be anything other than charming. 'I'll be there.'

'Great! I'll email your receptionist our address. Leigh is really looking forward to meeting you. This is so exciting!'

'Well, it's high time I met him. We have quite a few details to iron out before this wedding can go ahead. I'll see you Friday.'

As soon as she stepped out of the front door, Jade pulled out her mobile phone. 'Kat, I need to ask you something. Did Ash have his penthouse suite when he was with Angela?'

'No, he didn't buy it till about a month before you started working for him. Why?'

'Oh, nothing really. Just checking on a little detail.'

'Oh my god, Jade. You've booked her as your planner! You have to keep me posted!'

'Well, she won't be our planner by Friday afternoon. And to be honest, I may well not be Ashley's fiancée by then, either!'

'Feel like you're skating on thin ice?'

'Very much so...but you know, there's something about this that just feels right. Deliciously wicked, but so very right!'

They both burst out laughing. 'You tell me the second you're free exactly what happened. I want every last detail,' Kat demanded.

'I promise!'

'Honey, Mrs Renry, our wedding planner, is coming over for lunch on Friday afternoon. Can you spare an hour to meet her? It'll make all the difference to how she goes ahead with our plans.'

'No problem. Just an hour. I've got the Tier contract to finalise late Friday.'

'Perfect. Just perfect.'

Ashley couldn't read her. Jade seemed happy enough, but it just wasn't like her to pass over the organisation of something to someone else. Not when she was so skilled at it herself.

'How did you come across this Mrs Renry? Yellow Pages?'

'No, she came highly recommended.' Jade turned her back to him and he couldn't read her face. 'I think I might just take a nap. Who'd have thought pregnancy was so demanding?'

Ashley watched her walk away. Damn it, she was so gorgeous! Ashley pinched himself. So, it was true: Jade Stirling would soon be his wife. One thing was for sure: she seemed to have really got involved with the wedding preparations.

When noon arrived on Friday, Jade said 'I'm just popping out to pick up some sushi for lunch with Mrs Renry. I'll meet you at home.'

'Don't be late!' he said, smiling as Jade batted her eyelashes at him. 'I don't want to be left alone with a wedding planner!'

'Wouldn't dream of it. This meeting is really important. She's dying to meet you, Ash.'

'Why? What have you told her?'

'Everything...and nothing. That's why she needs to meet you. So she can see why you're the love of my life, and why...' Jade walked away.

'And why, what? Jade?'

'And why I'm *not* the love of your life. So she can see why you find it impossible to say you love me.'

'Jade, it's none of her business! I hope you haven't said…'

But she was out the door.

Bloody hell, Jade! Ashley got up from his desk. It was none of the woman's damn business why he couldn't say those words. It's not as if he didn't feel it. Surely Jade knew that? Ashley did love her. He was sure of it. That giddy feeling in his belly whenever he looked at Jade. That was love, wasn't it? If so, then he loved her with every fibre of his being! But why the hell did he have to say it?

A quick glance at his watch, and he knew he had to get out the door.

'I'll be back in 90 minutes,' he said to Emilia as he stepped into the lift.

As he approached the front door of their penthouse suite, his mobile alerted him to a text:

Honey, I'm running a few minutes late. Can you entertain Mrs Renry till I get there?
Jade xxxx

Damn!

Ashley stepped inside and poured himself a gin and tonic. Day drinking was rare, but at this very moment the thought of entertaining a wedding planner was just not what he was in the mood for.

The doorbell rang and he swiftly walked to the far side of the room to answer it. Opening the door, he stood back to greet Mrs Renry. Both of their faces were stripped of blood.

'Angela.'

'Ashley.'

'What the hell are you doing here?' he snapped.

'I'm...there must be some mistake,' she fumbled looking at the address in her hands. 'I'm meant to be meeting Jade and Leigh. I, I' she stumbled over her words, '... plan weddings now.'

'Jade and *Leigh*?' Ashley didn't know whether to laugh or yell.

Jade Stirling, this time you've gone too far!

'Come in!' he snapped. 'You're at the right place, but you're sure as hell not planning my wedding!'

'Where's Jade? Does she know that you and I were once lovers?'

'I've no idea, but we'll soon find out! Drink?' he asked, heading to the mini-bar.

'I think I need one. I had no idea. I'd never have taken on this wedding if I knew.'

'Of course you would! You wouldn't know love it if it slapped you on the face, but you know all about business. Shrewd, hard business deals. That's you all over, isn't it Angela?'

'There's no need to be so harsh. How long has it been, Ash? Nine years?'

'Nine years, and two months.'

'Counting?'

'Grateful for every day that you're not in my life!'

'Are you still sore about Tom? You know he was just a bit of fun on the side. You were always too busy at work to...fully satisfy my needs. Honestly, it was nothing personal.'

'This isn't about Tom, and you know it. Have your

135

drink and leave. We won't be requiring your services.'

'But Jade signed a contract.'

'I'm sure if Jade signed a contract there'll be a get-out clause somewhere. She's not stupid!' And he couldn't help grin at the thought of Jade and contracts. Many, many times she'd saved his butt by making something iron-clad. To the world she might have been just a PA, but there was a sharp legal brain behind that pretty face, which didn't miss a trick.

'Leave.'

'You wanted me to love you back, Ashley, and I didn't. At least I was honest. I would happily have married you, had your babies and whatever else you wanted. It would have been a good business decision for both of us. You know that. But love was never going to happen for me. It was always about me, and never about you. I'm too selfish to love anyone, but letting you go was the biggest mistake of my life. I'm not even in love with my husband. It's purely business, but it works for us. You're a good man, and Jade is very lucky. She's lucky to have a man who loves her so much.'

'Out!' There was no point continuing the conversation while he was so angry. No, not angry. Furious.

'Goodbye Ashley. I wish you well.'

Ashley refused to look in her direction. As soon as the door closed, he called Jade. 'Please leave a message, I'll get back to you as soon as I can!' her voice said sweetly. Ashley wanted to be angry at her instructions to leave a voicemail, but everything about her had the opposite effect on him. Just hearing her voice calmed his heart rate.

Where the hell was Jade? He had an important meeting to get back to. For half an hour he paced the living room, and then headed back to the office. He'd deal with Jade later.

Ashley could barely focus during his meeting. Angela's face haunted him. *What the hell was Jade thinking?* Angela was the last person in the world he wanted anything to do with. Did Jade think he still had a thing for her? That he still fancied her? Surely she wasn't jealous of Angela, too?

Jade decided to take in an afternoon movie, and then a stroll through the park. It was best to give Ashley a bit of cooling-down time before they met up. As for Angela, at some time they'd have to meet and terminate their contract. 100% refund had never felt so good!

Finally, she came home with an armload of vegetables and prepared to make a tasty meal of aubergine goulash. There wouldn't be any wine for her, but she chilled some sparkling white for Ashley. A nice home-cooked dinner, that's just what they needed. They'd had too many meals out lately. It was easy to lose touch with home life when they were being waited on night and day.

When she heard the key turn in the lock, she held her breath. Would he be angry? Furious? Worse, would he call off the wedding?

'Ah, honey. You're home. I've been worried about you. Did you track down that sushi?' he asked kindly.

'I'm so sorry. I got back here and you were gone. How was...'

'Mrs Renry seems more than up to the job. Clearly she has a lot of experience in the business world. Tell me again, how did you find her?'

Their eyes met. Who would keep up their poker

face the longest? Neither of them relented, and stared each other out.

'Um, she came recommended.' Jade couldn't read him. This wasn't the reaction she expected.

'Take time off work if you need to, but I don't want anyone else involved in planning our wedding. This is our day.'

'You didn't like her?' Jade asked incredulously.

That's it? He wasn't even going to mention that Angela was once part of his life? Not a single sentence about how they'd been lovers? About how she broke his heart? Jade wanted to throw something at him. Anything. How dare he act as if Angela was a complete stranger. That damn woman was all that was standing between her and Ashley declaring his love for Jade.

'Ashley, can I remind you that this is a business arrangement? A debt-collection plan! I don't see what the problem is. You were the one who said not to have a registry wedding. Make up your mind. What do you want? A full-on society wedding or a low-key heartless registry signing?'

'I want something special. I want you, and I want our wedding to be beautiful. I don't want that woman to be part of our lives. End of story. And Jade, this isn't up for discussion anymore. Mrs Renry is not going to be part of our wedding. Is that clear?'

Hell Hath No Fury

Jade had taken a bit longer for lunch than usual. There was so much work on at the moment, what with wedding preparations and the Serafina Simmo tour, not to mention trying to schedule in visits to Ashley's ailing mum, that taking an hour for lunch was a form of therapeutic solitude; not that it was quiet on the streets of London. Every two seconds, she wanted to whisk off her high heels; and then escape the pavement and crowds for five minutes. The park was busy with mothers and toddlers, but she tuned out the children's fussy cries, and let her bare feet touch the grass. Ah, that's better, she thought.

All morning she'd been annoyed by Leonie Allan hanging about Ashley's office. There was no reason for that woman to be anywhere near him. In fact, she should have been on the second floor in her department. Why was the woman hovering about? Jade knew that there was no reason to be jealous, but she couldn't let it go. There was nothing for it: she would tell Ashley that if the marriage was going to happen, then Leonie would have to leave. Ashley had already admitted that the women didn't do anything other than paint fingernails and send texts. Jade had added: *and usually both at the same time!*

They were due to fly to India in three weeks to meet up with Serafina, and Jade found herself feeling grateful that they'd be away from Leonie, even if just for a few days. She tried to dismiss her increasing angst as just pregnancy hormones.

'Why is Ashley's door shut?' Jade asked Emilia as she entered the reception area. 'He doesn't have any appointments till 3pm.'

Emilia looked across to Hannah.

'Leonie Allan. She insisted that she needed a personal meeting.'

Both women knew it was the worst thing they could have said to Jade, and waited for the bomb to explode. Ashley Lyndhurst had an open-door policy, and for it to be closed could only mean one thing...

'Did she just?'

Jade unceremoniously stormed into Ashley's office without even a courtesy knock. What she did not expect to see was Leonie Allan perched on his side of the large mahogany desk, less than half a metre away from where he was sitting.

The look on Jade's face told Ashley he should be concerned.

'Jade!' he yelled as she spun out the door. 'Jade, get back here!'

'I won't be back in the office for the rest of the week. You can call it personal time!' Jade said as she walked past Emilia and Hannah and straight out the front door.

'Where is she?' Ashley asked as he entered the reception area. 'Where is she?!'

'Gone, sir. Jade said she wouldn't be in for the rest of the week.'

'Damn it!' Ashley ran down the stairs and out onto the street just as a black taxi was pulling away. 'Damn it Jade!'

Jade reflected on Leonie's highly inappropriate office manner and was furious that Ashley didn't send her straight out of his office at the first sign of flirting. It was far too busy a time for her to call in sick days, but there was no way she was going to hang around and watch

Leonie's coup! Ashley was *her* fiancé, not Leonie's! Jade knew that she needed a plan, and she needed it quickly.

The taxi driver pulled up outside the lilac-coloured building, and within minutes Jade was being escorted into a room.

'I don't have an appointment booked for today, but I'm desperate,' she pleaded.

'We happen to have a vacancy, Jade. Must be your lucky day.'

This had become her weekly pampering ritual: reflexology, Indian head massage, and Swedish massage.

As her cares melted away beneath the tender hands of Suzie, and the strains of Enya on the stereo, Jade's mind became laser like. If Ashley Lyndhurst was so fond of Leonie Allan, he could damn well marry her! And there, just like yeast and flour and sugar, the idea began to rise and rise and rise. Oh what a clever baker she was!

Feeling rejuvenated, relaxed and full of the wisdom of the Universe, Jade went back to the penthouse and started preparations. It was simple, really; only, why had she never thought of it before?

Facebook was such a wonderful tool, except when people used incorrect grammar and unforgiveable spelling. That, to her mind, was inexcusable.

Why had Ashley never had a fanpage? Surely a man so well-known and respected in the aviation industry—a friend to the stars, in fact—should have a social-media presence?

And that was her afternoon's work. *What a good PA*, she told herself.

Ashley Lyndhurst had a fan page tailor made to fit him and his lifestyle, and this just happened to include albums of photos that the poor soul had never seen before. Jade's mobile phone had been quite the repository of 'not for public consumption' photos: too much food in his mouth here, and a stumble up the stairs after a bottle of wine there. And then there was that impromptu naked swim he'd taken in the Waikato River in New Zealand one Summer. Amazing how she just happened to have the phone poised on his perfectly ripped torso as he stepped out of the water. It wasn't as if he said 'not for public consumption.' Ashley had just assumed that she'd delete it at some point; that is, after she'd finished laughing.

Jade could have kissed Kat a thousand times for emailing her the photo of Ash when he was fifteen years old: huge zit on his nose, and a haircut he'd attempted himself before a first date. There were no excuses for looking like that, no matter how handsome he was. And what about that one of him aged two years old? Squatting on his potty, straining to push out a poo; a photo that only a mother could truly love! Ashley's mother never even asked Jade why she wanted that photo. Bless Mrs Lyndhurst. Oh yes, she was going to be the perfect mother-in-law.

Jade plodded on all afternoon, routinely rejecting each and every call that Ashley made to her mobile phone.

In a moment of inspired genius, Jade scrolled through the office party photos from Christmas two years before: the one where *everyone* had too much to drink. Everyone, that is, except Jade.

Leonie had been so drunk that she'd collapsed on the floor, her reindeer antlers slipping across her face, and her wrists bound, by Jake the courier, in silver tinsel. Leonie had laughed so much that she ended up crying, and her mascara made her eyes equivalent to those of a Chinese panda.

'Ha ha my pretty,' Jade cackled as she popped the photo from her mobile onto the Facebook page. 'But you're so lovely Ms Allan that I won't put you into an album. Oh no, I couldn't possibly do that. We'll make you the very first status update on Ash's new page. You want to be close to MY Ashley, I'll put you close! Take that!'

Upload photo: Reindeer Chic.

Status update: Introducing the woman of my dreams, Leonie Allan.

And then came the final part of her afternoon's work. Requests to 'like' the page were sent to everyone at Lyndhurst, except Ashley and Leonie, of course; and to every airline company executive she'd ever liaised with. Then she sent it to her 567 Facebook friends, and her 4,000 Twitter followers.

Emilia was straight on the phone.

'You're wicked! Mr Lyndhurst won't want to marry you when he sees this. Are you nuts?'

'Possibly. Have you liked the page?'

'That page will have at least a thousand fans by the end of the day. Everyone in the office is sending it far and wide. But Jade, there's something you should know.'

'Yeah, what is it?'

'It's the reason Leonie was in the office this afternoon...'

'I don't want to know!'

'Oh yes you do.'

Jade's phone was constantly ringing, and she kept hitting reject. Between Emilia and Ashley's constant calls, she was going crazy. 'Turn the phone off,' she told herself, and sat down to a jumbo-sized tub of toffee ice cream and afternoon TV.

When Ashley came through the door she didn't take her eyes off the screen. 'Don't worry, I'll be out before the end of the week. Just need to sort some accommodation. I can't exactly move back to my apartment while it's being rented out. If you can't wait that long, I'll stay in a hotel,' she said, offering him some leeway. Not once did she look up at him.

'What the hell are you talking about?' Ashley ripped off his tie and threw it on the sofa. 'Jade, you have got to learn not to make assumptions! Why do you always think the worst of me? I don't understand it.'

That was the final straw.

'You think I just imagined her sitting on your desk? On *your* side of the desk, her legs practically rubbing up against yours? Practically around you like a boa constrictor? You think I *imagined* that?'

Jade stood up to her full height, her face red and angry, hands on her hips as if she was about to stamp her foot. 'I could smell her pheromones from the doorway! That was not an assumption or my imagination. Stop putting the blame on me!'

'Calm down Jade. It's not good for the baby when you get so upset.'

'Well this baby will have to learn exactly what sort of father they have!'

'Leonie was in my office because she was giving notice. She has a new job, and she was sitting so close to me because she was grovelling. You know what she's like! Of course it was inappropriate, but it wasn't me who was in the wrong. She wants to start her new job straight away and was buttering me up to let her out of the contract. Oddly, I thought you'd be delighted that she was leaving at long last. Sometimes I just can't figure you out, Jade. You never used to be like this. What happened?'

You happened, is what she wanted to say. *You turned my head to mush. You make me unable to think rationally. You, damn it, you!*

Jade looked up at him. How many fans did he have on Facebook now, she wondered as she took in his dark, wavy hair, and strong jawline. Would they be so understanding of his dilemma? Bloody hell!

She had to get that page down, and pronto. How the heck could she get rid of him so she could go online?

'Well, why don't you go and have a shower and I'll sort us some dinner?' she said, hoping for a lifeline. The colour was rapidly leaving her face.

'No, I'm fine. I'll have one later. Shall we go out for dinner?'

Why was he being so calm? It was unnerving.

One thing was clear: he would not be calm when he realised her latest antic. Nope, not calm at all. It could well be the last straw. It might be the very thing that makes him realise she's not worth his time.

'Well, maybe you should go for a walk and get some fresh air. It's always a good antidote to being cooped up in the office all day.'

'You seem particularly concerned about my welfare all of a sudden.'

'Yes,' she said, but realised there was nothing more she could add. How the hell was she going to get online?

'Why don't you come for a walk with me?'

'Me?'

'Yes, you. Pregnant women need to exercise too.'

145

'Sure,' she said, reluctantly agreeing. 'I just need to make a call. Can you give me a minute?'

'Of course.'

Jade picked up her mobile and walked into the bedroom, firmly closing the door behind her. Jade didn't hear Ashley laugh, or see him when he opened his iPhone and logged into Facebook. And she didn't see him comment on his new fan page.

Nor did she see the three-dozen photos he posted there detailing Jade's alfalfa adventures, her spot of tie-dyeing and tailor work. And neither did she read his comments: *Hell hath no fury like a Jade Stirling scorned. Given the choice, who would you marry? Leonie Reindeer-Come-Panda Allan or Jade Alfalfa Stirling?*

Within a few minutes, his comment already had four hundred likes, and eighty comments. Most of them came from men saying that Jade was one very scary woman, and he'd better have insurance if he planned to live with her for the rest of his life.

'Emilia, you have to get rid of the fan page for me. I can't get to it now. The password is: jaded! With an exclamation mark. Just delete the bloody thing. Gotta go.'

Jade slapped her cheeks gently to bring the blood back to them. The ghost look just wasn't convincing when you wanted to appear on top of things. Before she left the bedroom, she grabbed a coat and then greeted Ashley with a smile.

'Everything okay?' he asked, linking his arm into hers.

'Yep,' she said.

They wandered through Hyde Park, and eventually came to sit on a park bench.

'So, have you forgiven me yet?' he asked.

'What for?' she replied, her mind AWOL in the heady, addictive blue colour of Facebook and friends.

'Leonie on my desk.'

'Oh, yes, of course. All forgotten. I'm sorry I....'

'Sorry for what, Jade?'

'Nothing.'

Jade's phone alerted her to a text from Emilia: *Can't delete, it's too funny. Page has three thousand fans. Gone bloody viral because of those photos. Sorry! Nonstop comments from around the world.*

'Shit!' Jade muttered under her breath.

'What is it honey?'

'Nothing. Little matter at the office I need to sort out. You stay here and enjoy the fresh air.'

'Not so fast, Jade Stirling. Not so fast!' Ashley guided her back to the park bench. 'How many fans do I have now?' Ashley tried his best not laugh, but the look on her face was worth more than his entire fleet of planes.

'You *know*?'

'How many?'

'3,000' she said, cringing into the sleeve of her coat and hiding her face. 'I'm so…'

'Don't apologise, Jade. Funnily enough, it might actually be good for business. I'm surprised you didn't create a page for me sooner.'

'How can it be good for business? Have you seen those photos?'

Ashley laughed out loud. 'Honey, I've seen everything. The photos show that I'm human, and that I have some pretty crazy women in my life. Oddly, people relate to that. Don't ask me why, but they do. If there's anything I've learnt about you lately, it is that you're good for me. You're good at helping me not take life so seriously. I think you deserve a pay rise.'

'But you're always so fussy about your reputation and about being professional. Aren't you angry with me?'

'I was, at first. I was angrier than I've been since the day I discovered the sprout factory in my penthouse. But then I realised that the more you keep doing these crazy things, the more I'll be able to hold them against you. You'll be indebted to me for a very long time, Ms Stirling. It's perfect ammunition as far as I'm concerned.'

'Oh,' she said. 'Oh.'

Goodbye

They were bickering about the wedding date and location when the phone rang.

'Yes, sure. I'll be there straight away.' Ashley turned to face Jade and said 'Mum's ill. Well, even more ill than she's been. My sisters said I should come back straight away. Can you come up to the farm with me?'

'How ill?'

'Very. Are you coming?'

'Now? Yes, of course. If you think it's appropriate. Shouldn't it just be family?'

'Jade, you are family. My mother adores you, and so do my sisters.'

And do you adore me, Ashley? The words were keening off her tongue. Two weeks on from his meeting with Angela, and he still hadn't said a word about their relationship.

They could have used one of his small planes to fly to Cumbria, it would have been quicker, but Ashley needed time to process the news. His mother's health had been unstable for some time, but he had no idea of the severity of the illness. Jade always passed on her messages, and pencilled him into the diary for weekend visits where possible, but he'd dismissed his mother's flailing energy levels to age and overdoing it on the farm. It had been four weeks since his last visit, and she'd deteriorated hugely in that time.

Most of the journey up the motorway was taken in silence. Jade's new silver Peugeot cabriolet purred along the bitumen, breathlessly passing other motorists. Beyond the Howgills, they neared to Copperhill Farm, a small but thriving organic vegetable-box business now run primarily by Ashley's sisters.

Ashley tooted the horn as the tyres crunched on the white-pebble driveway. His twin, Arabella, was the first to run out of the large sandstone farmhouse, closely followed by his sisters Katrina and Kirsty. There were solemn hugs all around, and Arabella led him by the hand up the steps.

'Jade, how are things doing? I heard there was a bit of a betting nightmare at the office?' Kirsty giggled.

'You know about that?' she gasped, horrified that her life was common knowledge. 'Emilia fills me in on everything I should know about. I bet for my brother bringing you home,' she smiled, squeezing Jade's hand tighter.

'You *did*?'

'Of course I did. He's been pining for you for years. The idiot just didn't know it. We always laughed that he couldn't even come home here for a weekend without needing to bring his PA. How could one man be so blind? Jade, he needed you to be gone to have his eyes opened. Well done!' Her giggle was shorter this time. 'Mum's really sick. The doctor says it's just a matter of time now.'

'It's that bad? Why didn't you say?'

'Mum didn't want Ash disturbed.'

'But...'

'I know. I know. But they were her wishes. He's here now, that's all that matters.'

'I really shouldn't be here. Perhaps I'll wait in the car. This is family time.'

'Jade Stirling! You *are* family. Tell me a Christmas you and your mother haven't shared with us in the past seven years? Tell me which of our family get-togethers you haven't been part of?' Katrina asked.

Jade breathed in deeply.

'Kat, this is different. This is…'

'Shhh. Mum wants to see you. She's been asking after you.'

Mrs Lyndhurst's eyes lit up when her only son entered the room. 'My boy,' she whispered, taking his hand. Ashley was taken aback. She really *was* ill. Ashley held her pale hand in his, and listened to her laboured breathing. How come he'd not been informed? The sight of her balding head and sallow skin shook him to the core. Here she was, fighting for her life, and he'd been so engrossed in *his* life that he hadn't even taken the time to tell her about the recent awards or their pregnancy. It's not as if the news wasn't common knowledge but he could have kicked himself for the omission.

'I saw your awards in the paper, son. I'm so proud of you.'

Ashley searched his sisters' eyes desperate for some sort of confirmation. Was their mother as ill as she looked?

'Jade dear, it's so nice to see you. Thank you for coming. I'm at peace now. I've waited for this for a long time. It's good to know that Ash has you by his side. I feel so much better knowing that.'

They sat for some time making small talk, and then Ashley leaned over and whispered to his mother 'Jade and I are having a baby.'

'A baby? That's wonderful news. I'm so happy.'

As the next few days seeped into each other, it became apparent that Mrs Lyndhurst wouldn't see next week. Discreetly calling the office several times, Jade made arrangements with Emilia to postpone various meetings, and updated her on contracts which needed signing but could be delayed until their return.

'I guess the wedding plans will be delayed for a bit?' Emilia asked.

'It's the furthest thing from my mind right now, and I imagine it is for Ashley as well. We've barely said a word to each other the past few days.'

'Fancy a walk?' Ashley asked Jade later that afternoon. 'I could do with some fresh air, and your company.'

'Sure,' she said, reaching for his hand. 'I'm so sorry that your mother is dying.'

'I know you are.'

They walked in silence for several minutes.

'Tell her you love her before it's too late,' she urged him.

'Are you talking about my mother or about you?' he asked, his eyes trying to find an oasis in hers.

'Both. We both need to hear it. Stop punishing me for what that woman did. It's not fair. I don't deserve it, and your mother certainly doesn't either.'

'Drop it, Jade. You don't know what you're talking about.'

'I'm not Angela Nightingale, so stop making me pay for what she did to you!'

'Don't do this. Not now. Not while all this is going on. Your timing is lousy, Jade. Absolutely lousy.'

'Is it? When is the right time to tell someone you love them?'

'I didn't come out here to fight with you. I asked you to come for a walk because right now I need you. My sisters are going to fall apart when Mum dies, and I might have to spend some time up here. I need to know that you'll be with me.'

'If you want me by your side, then that's where I'll be. The same as I always have. Nothing's changed.'

'Good.' They walked in silence for some time. Eventually, he reached for her hand and said 'I'm sorry. I don't like it when we argue.'

The setting Sun splashed its apricot-infused rays over the organic smallholding, and the day's end seemed symbolic of the finale now facing the Lyndhurst family. What lay over the horizon?

Tears trickled down Jade's face as she watched Ashley and his sisters hold their mother's hands. Final breaths relieved themselves from her body, and without fuss she left this world behind and slipped over the horizon alongside the Sun.

Jade felt powerless to support Ashley in his grief. In all their years together, she'd never seen him cry before. Ashley Lyndhurst was always so strong, and so capable. When he eventually lifted his head, their eyes met, and a thousand words passed between them. Everything inside him called to her: *be with me, Jade*.

Jade tiptoed over and put her arms around him, whispering in his dark hair: *I love you. I'm so sorry*. No one left the room that afternoon. Kat and Kirsty brushed Mrs Lyndhurst's hair, and Arabella washed down her body with water and herbs. At Mrs Lyndhurst's request, she'd be buried on the farm, beside her late husband, in nothing more than a cloth shroud: a simple ceremony for a woman who loved to be in nature.

Replacement

The next few weeks were spent at the farm with the adult Lyndhurst children easing each other through the biggest transition of their lives. Jade managed a fair amount of her work from there, but every few days flew from Carlisle to London to oversee office management. They had the India trip looming, and she had to make a judgment call about whether Ash would be able to join her. First and foremost, he needed time to grieve and she didn't want to drag him from that process prematurely.

Jade was sorting through the huge pile of mail on Ashley's desk when she noticed dozens of envelopes with personal addresses on the back. As she continued dividing the mail into piles: bills, invoices, promotional, industry magazines, *personal*, she became suspicious. *And what the hell was that pink smelly envelope all about?*

Unceremoniously, she ripped it open to reveal a handwritten CV and application for PA to the chief executive. A frown burrowed into her forehead. At first she wondered if the letter had been delayed in the post and was meant to arrive at the time she moved to Australia. For a while, her fingers fiddled with the paper and gum of several more envelopes; all the same: CVs and applications to be Ashley Lyndhurst's PA.

For the next half hour or so, she stomped around his office. Why hadn't he told her that he was advertising for a new PA? What about all his promises that she could do the same job from home? Had he lied to her? He may have just lost his darling mother, but Jade was not putting up with this. No way!

Jade scooped up the entire collection of job applications and calmly headed back to her office.

'I'm not to be disturbed, Emilia.'

Emilia laughed. 'Should I be worried?'

Jade smiled at her. The girl knew her far too well!

Three hours, that's what it took to reply to each and every one. Jade did them the courtesy of not sending out standard replies but making each one personal. Afterwards, she placed a bunch of Lyndhurst Incorporated letterheads into the printer tray. And then she hit print:

Dear Janelle,

Thank you for your CV and application to be the PA for Ashley Lyndhurst.

The position requires someone who is able to work six days a week, to travel at a moment's notice, and who can coordinate Mr Lyndhurst's diary and schedule appointments internationally.

Mr Lyndhurst requires someone who can also work Sundays if the need arises which usually happens at least once a fortnight. You will need an up-to-date passport, clean driver's licence, current first-aid certificate, a great appetite for sushi, and to provide Mr Lyndhurst with home-grown alfalfa sprouts each Monday morning.

If you can meet the above requirements, you are invited to attend an interview on September 26th at 5pm. Please bring a sample of your sprouts, and the original, above-stated documents. Should you be

unable to attend the appointment, please
email me in the first instance.

Jade Stirling
PA to Ashley Lyndhurst

The two things that all the letters had in common were: to bring alfalfa sprouts, and to arrive at 5pm on September 26th.

As Jade left the office building that evening, her arm loaded with mail, Emilia asked 'Why do you have that look of a cat that has just eaten a mouse? Should Ashley be scared?'

'I have; and yes he should.'

Ashley arrived back at work for September 26th, and settled into office life rather quickly. 'Jade,' he called down the phone, 'Can you come in here?'

Seconds later, she was in his office.

'What's wrong?'

'Is this all the mail there is?'

'Yes. Is that all you wanted me for?'

'Yes,' he said, flipping through the envelopes, confused that there were no applications for the advertised PA role.

'Okay,' she walked back to her office with a smile on her face. So, he wasn't going to tell her that he'd advertised *her* job?

Not a single applicant had contacted her to say that they were declining an interview. According to her records that meant that Ashley Lyndhurst could look forward to no less than 36 interviews at precisely 5pm that afternoon. Ah, yes, life was good as his PA.

At 4pm Jade popped her head around the door to

Ashley's office. 'You know, I've got the sudden urge to visit my mum. I think I'll spend the weekend with her. Mind if I leave early?'

'In Devon? All weekend?' he asked. 'That came out of nowhere.' Ashley stood up and walked over to her. 'Are you alright? Is there anything you want to tell me? I know we've not spent much time together lately; not much private time, that is, without my sisters around, but if anything's wrong, you know you can tell me, right?'

'And you know you can tell me anything, right?' she asked, pinning him down with her chocolate-coloured eyes.

Nothing. Not a thing! Right, mate, she said to herself, *Devon it is.*

'Just missing my mum. Haven't seen her in months. See you Monday.' Jade was about to walk away, when he pulled her back to him by the wrist, far more firmly than he intended to.

'You're not even going to kiss me goodbye?' he asked suspiciously.

'Must have slipped my mind,' she said, biting her lip.

'Jade, what's going on?'

'Nothing. Really.' Jade stood up on tiptoes and kissed him on the cheek. Time was marching on and she had to get out of the office.

Ashley pulled her in closer to him, and settled for no less than a slow, long, intimate kiss. To hell with being in view of Hannah and Emilia. To hell with it! As his tongue sought hers, and he hungrily consumed her, he wanted to make sure that she thought of him, and of that kiss, every single second while she was gone. Jade's body responded in kind, and for a heartbeat he almost made her forget that she needed to leave the office.

Jade's legs began to wobble. Ashley Lyndhurst still had the ability to make her lose her balance. As she lifted her palms to his chest she said 'I really want to get going before the traffic builds up. Have a lovely weekend, Ashley. I've left a casserole in the fridge for you.'

'Maybe I could come with you?'

No you can't! That's what she wanted to yell, but she smiled sweetly. 'No honey, you don't need a weekend of my mother going on about baby booties and names that have been in our family for generations. You just have a peaceful weekend at home.'

And before he had a chance to reply she was out the door, with nothing more than a wave.

Emilia and Hannah looked at each other. Then they looked at the clock. If only they could leave early.

At 4.50pm, several ladies entered the foyer, and within minutes the room was filled to capacity as a few dozen applicants for the role of PA waited for their interview. Ashley walked out of his office to find out what all the commotion was coming from the waiting area. In a moment of déjà vu, he felt his pulse quicken. There was far too much alfalfa in a non-food area to be comfortable with. What the hell was going on?

'Emilia, my office. Now.' He spoke softly, and looked her firmly in the eye.

Emilia had followed him in, wishing she could hit speed dial on her phone and ask Jade what the hell was going on. But she knew exactly what was going on: Jade must have discovered that Ashley had advertised her job.

'What are all those women doing in there? And more importantly, why are they all carrying large trays and bags of alfalfa sprouts? Is this some kind of sick joke?'

'Ashley, hand on heart, I know nothing about this. I promise you. What I imagine has happened is that Jade must have found out you'd advertised her job.'

Ashley sat back in his leather chair, and swung it around to the look at the city skyline.

'The truth is, I am going to need someone once she's at home with the baby. I know she can do a lot of work from home, but she won't be able to do everything.'

'Well, then I suggest you get interviewing these women; sample their sprouts,' she chuckled, 'and find yourself a bloody good Jade Stirling replacement!'

'Is that actually possible?' he laughed. 'Why are they all here at the same time? Why weren't their appointments scheduled across the day? Actually, across the week? There are so many of them!'

'I'd love to help you out, sir, but I've got plans and need to leave at five. Sorry.'

Ashley rubbed his eyes, and said 'Fine. I'll deal with them. Have a nice weekend.'

If he interviewed them one at a time, he'd be here all night. The only thing he really wanted to do was go home and have a stiff drink. No, what he really wanted to do was go home and make love with Jade. Damn her! When he thought of her, he realised that she'd probably be laughing all the way to Devon!

'Right, ladies. We're going to do this in alphabetical order. So, if your surname begins with A through to G, then please come into my office.'

Twelve women, tottering on high heels, and twelve lots of alfalfa sprouts, paraded into his office. The stench of perfume reminded him of Leonie Allan. And a small laugh escaped his lips. He wondered, for just a second, if Jade had instructed them to wear their finest perfume for the interview! It wouldn't have surprised him if she did.

To his great surprise, however, he managed the evening well. Within seconds of meeting each of the women, he ascertained that none of them would be adequate for the job; however, he invited five of them back for a second interview first thing on Monday morning. The interview, he told them, would be conducted by his PA, Jade Stirling, at 7am in their penthouse.

Before leaving the office that night, he placed every bag, basket and tray of sprouts on Jade's desk. She liked alfalfa.

The weekend dragged on and on, and despite burying his head in industry magazines and phoning his sisters every few hours, life just didn't feel right without Jade by his side. Everywhere in his life were signs to show him that they were meant to be together, and at every turn he was always pushing her away by his non-committal attitude to love.

At 3am on Monday, Ashley was awoken by Jade crawling into bed.

'What time is it?'

'Three. Car had a flat tyre. I should have been home last night. Shhh. I need my sleep.'

Ashley wrapped his arms around her, and whispered into her ear.

'You should have called. I'd have come and picked you up.'

Pretty soon, he realised his words were wasted. Jade was already fast asleep. It felt so good to have her back in his arms. He never wanted her to leave again. And even though they had a baby coming into the equation, he was determined they'd find a way to make it work so they could spend every possible moment together. Ashley breathed in the scent of jasmine and vanilla: Jade, *his* Jade; and kissed her head. Thank God she was back. Tomorrow they'd finally set a wedding date.

Tomorrow arrived far quicker than either of them anticipated, with thunderous storms lashing across the city, spiky raindrops splintering against the windows demanding they start the new work week. Ashley staggered into the kitchen, wearing nothing but his black silk Boxer shorts; his long, toned legs evidence of a man who put time into caring for his body through daily workouts. While the coffee brewed, he picked up The Guardian newspaper from outside his front door.

Jade yawned as she entered the kitchen.

'I've squeezed you an orange juice,' Ashley said proudly, passing her the glass.

'Thanks. I'm so tired. Mind if I go in to work an hour or so later?'

'Take your time,' he smiled, wrapping his arms around her. 'It's so good to have you home. It felt like you were away for weeks.'

The intercom buzzed, and Ashley said 'Bit early for visitors.'

'I'll get it,' Jade answered, walking to the door in

nothing but a sexy lingerie.

'Who is it?' she asked through the intercom.

'My name is Jessie. I'm here for the interview.'

Jade turned to Ashley in confusion.

'Must be for you,' he said, picking up his newspaper and walking to the sofa.

'Are you at least going to put some clothes on before I open the door?' she asked.

'No,' he said, making himself comfortable. He placed the paper on the coffee table, and took a sip of his coffee.

Jade opened the door, completely self-conscious about her unbrushed hair and clothing of choice.

'Hi,' she said, taken aback to see several women outside her door.

'I'm afraid I had a late night, and I'm not quite ready. Why don't you come and join Mr Lyndhurst for a coffee while I go and get changed?' she said, ushering them all in to the open-plan living area. She winked at Ashley on her way to the bedroom.

'Ladies, good morning. My apologies for Jade being so disorganised. Take a seat,' he said, gesturing to the three spare sofas. 'Coffee, anyone?'

Each of the women looked at each other in a silent solidarity: oddest interview ever, their eyes acknowledged.

Ashley's lean muscles were taut, and with each step towards the kitchen he heard light mews and moans. *This is going to be fun*, he chuckled to himself. He could hear Jade in the shower, so he knew she wasn't going to be out anytime in the next couple of minutes.

'Milk? Cream? Sugar? Honey?' he called out, and then prepared to make each of the coffees to order.

Carefully carrying the tray to the lounge, Ash

placed it down on the table, and stood in front of them. Staring at the boss's body had to be taboo, right? Four of the five women kept their heads down, staring endlessly into the coffee in their hands. One of them, Natasha, kept her eyes on Ashley the whole time as she looked him up and down, and with laser-like precision hunted him down with just her eyes.

'Mr Lyndhurst, your wife must be a very secure person to let you entertain potential PAs while wearing nothing but your underwear.'

Ashley chuckled. 'I'm afraid I had a late night, and completely forgot about these interviews. I can assure you, I would prefer to be wearing a suit right now.'

'Don't let us stop you from getting dressed, Mr Lyndhurst.' The way she said those words reminded him of Leonie and he hoped like hell that Jade wouldn't want him to employ her. Ashley casually strolled to his bedroom, fully aware that his body was on full display and that every muscle was being examined, and passed Jade as she stepped out of the ensuite. Despite her exhaustion, she looked professional in her ankle-length, navy skirt and white blouse. Ash reached for her hand, and then pulled her in close. He'd show those women just whose body he wanted. Within seconds, Jade was whirled into his arms, and buried beneath his lips.

'I want you now,' he whispered, and then let her go. 'You're utterly gorgeous.' Ashley left her there, breathless, and headed for the shower.

Jade's face was flushed as she circled in towards her applicants. 'Thank you so much for coming here this morning ladies. I'm sorry for being disorganised. The car broke down en route from Devon last night, and I'm short of several hours sleep. Right, let's see, where shall we start?' Within minutes she'd ascertained their names, and linked them visually to the CVs they'd sent in. Natasha belonged to the pink envelope and perfume. Not a chance in hell that she'd make a third interview. What was it about her that made her think of Leonie?

Karen was sweet, but too shy. The position required someone with fortitude and gumption. Alissa had a severe stutter. She'd be excellent at many aspects of the job, expect the most important one: clear communication with clients, worldwide.

Lizzie's CV had read like a dramatic novel. Too unstable. Why the hell did Ashley narrow her down to the final five? There was no obvious reason for his choice.

Margarita was a pretty Spanish immigrant, with an excellent grasp of language, but wasn't a speed typist. Her smile was fetching, and Jade wondered if that's why he picked her.

Ashley emerged after what Jade considered the longest shower in history, wearing a new suit. Actually, they were all new suits, she reminded herself.

Nice tie, she thought to herself, admiring the purple flowers set against the black silk and making a mental note to go and buy him some more ties. Surely he must be missing his old ones?

Ashley joined her on the sofa, and asked 'How's it all going?'

'Each of these women would be perfect for the role. I'm afraid the choice is going to have to be yours, Ashley. I can't decide.'

None of them were suitable; they both knew that Ashley simply set up this arrangement to pay her back for the most recent alfalfa invasion!

'Perhaps we should give all of them a job?' he

said, catching Jade's eyes. 'After all, it would take five women to do the job you do.'

'Yes it would,' she admitted. 'I'm glad you realise.' Jade smiled, and then thanked the ladies for their time and promised they'd be in touch within the next forty-eight hours.

Natasha looked Ashley up and down, her eyes hungry for more of his skin. Jade felt herself gasp at the audacity of the woman!

When they were all out of the door, Ashley grabbed her by the wrist and said 'Any more surprises, Ms Stirling?'

'You tell me!'

Jade stormed into the bedroom and grabbed her handbag.

'Why are you angry at me?' he yelled.

'Did you see the way Natasha looked at you? Like, like...like you were there for the taking?'

'And that's my fault, how?'

'I can't stand this. I can't bear women looking at you like they just have to bat their eyelids and they'll be in your bed. It drives me crazy.'

'I guess she won't be my new PA then?' a small smile dared to touch his lips, and he grabbed his brief case. 'Let's go out for breakfast before we head into the office. Come on,' he said, grabbing her hand and kissing it.

'Stop buttering me up, Lyndhurst. I'm not in the mood.'

'Wouldn't dream of it, Ms Stirling. Wouldn't dream of it.'

Twenty minutes later, they were in Covent Garden dining at *Balthazar*, a brassiere, being served brioche with smoked salmon and scrambled egg. The setting was upmarket, and all the diners were smartly dressed. Despite reservations being difficult to book, Ashley Lyndhurst merely had to turn up at the door and he'd be ushered in. *Balthazar*, with antiqued mirrored walls, beautiful mosaic floors, its red awnings and plush red-leather banquettes, was his favourite place to dine for breakfast, and Ashley often held business meetings here. In fact, he and Jade had eaten here so many times that it was like a home away from home. The plan was to put her in a good mood before they went to the office.

'Honey, do you trust me?' he asked her when she'd finished eating. 'Do you trust me to be faithful to you?'

'I don't know. As far as I'm concerned, it seems like we're just together so I can pay off a debt.'

'And funnily enough, you just keep adding to that debt which makes me believe that you never want to be rid of me. Cute trick on Friday afternoon, by the way, leaving me with an office full of desperate women. I'm not going to forget that little stunt anytime soon.' He reached for her hand. 'I'm here for the long haul, Jade. I'm not going anywhere. You have to trust me.'

'We need to get to work,' she said, aborting the conversation with her last mouthful of tomato juice.

The work week felt like wading through treacle. Jade's mind wasn't on the job. Any decent PA could do the job, but they wouldn't be able to do it as well as she did. If he was happy to settle for less, then he'd be able to employ someone in no time. Jade would be redundant in every sense of the word. Although her heart ached to be a stay-at-home mother, when she thought of long days away from Ashley her heart ached just as much. How would she ever balance the two?

Let Me Fly

'It's just not the right time for a wedding, Ash. Let's leave it for a while. Your family has a lot of healing to do.'

'Jade, you're wrong. For once, you're wrong. It's the perfect time. This wedding is a celebration of our relationship, and that we're becoming a family. It's an acknowledgement that life goes on. Mum would have wanted that. She'd hate that we delayed this because she died.'

Jade decided not to argue. If this was what he wanted, then he could have the wedding. And until he found it within himself to say he loved her, then the marriage was nothing more than a debt-repayment plan. The sooner she got used to the reality of that, the better.

It was late on an autumnal Sunday afternoon when Jade suggested they take a walk by the river. 'Come on, let's get some fresh air.'

Surprised that he didn't argue, or claim that he had paperwork to look over, Jade decided that he seemed rather mellow. It had been three weeks since his mother's funeral, and they'd only been back in London for a short time.

Canadian geese flew overhead, and the crisp air invigorated Ashley and Jade. Rugged up in an ivory-coloured, cable-knit jumper, paired with faded-denim jeans, he looked so handsome Jade thought her heart would melt. 'Honey, you look gorgeous. I could just…'

'Could you now?' he laughed. 'It's a bit cold out here for me to be ripping your clothes off.'

'Oh, mine can stay on. It's yours that I want off!'

It was the first time in weeks, the first time since Mrs Lyndhurst's funeral, that they'd managed to laugh. Hand in hand, they walked amongst the copper, mustard and aubergine-coloured leaves.

'Talk to me about Angela.' Jade knew that she was asking for trouble by bringing that woman into a perfectly vibrant Autumn afternoon, but the words tripped off her tongue before she had a chance to lasso them into submission.

'My relationship, if that's what it could be called, with Angela ended about two years before I met you. I'd dated other women before her. Nice women! What it was about Angela, I couldn't honestly tell you. She was a hard-nosed business woman, and so ambitious it was scary. But, in a way, I found it quite fascinating to see a woman with that much drive.'

'But when I was ambitious, you tried to cut me off at the knees. Why was that?'

Ashley looked her in the eyes and simply said, 'I didn't want to lose you. I knew you'd go far, and I couldn't bear the thought of you not being part of my world.'

'But it was okay for Angela to reach the sky?'

'It's only looking back that I can see it's because I didn't feel the same about her as I do with you, and that the attraction was based on her drive, and nothing else.'

'And Tom?' she asked.

Ashley could only guess that his sisters had been telling tales behind his back.

'Tom and Angela had been together for years. Since school, apparently. I was too busy building up my business to even notice that she spent more time with him than with me. Or maybe I did, and partly felt relief. Angela is quite a harsh woman.'

'You don't say!' Jade laughed, rolling her eyes in disgust.

'When I found them in bed together, I should have walked away then and there, but I felt strangely grateful to Tom that he was looking after her!'

'I don't understand how you can have anything to do with that man. I would have...'

Ashley laughed out loud. 'I hate to think of what you'd have done to him, given what you did to my home when I didn't do anything.'

'Exactly,' she smiled.

The both laughed, and spontaneously hugged each other.

'I'm sorry they hurt you so much,' she whispered after he finished kissing her.

'It was for the best.'

'How can you say that? What they did was cruel. Look at how much it has impacted on you.'

'I was about to propose to her. I told Angela I loved her, and she made a mockery of it. The truth was...' He stopped talking. How could he even begin to share this with Jade? 'I didn't love Angela. I told her I did, but I didn't. I have no idea why I even said it! I'm grateful that she laughed in my face. I wasn't traumatised, I was relieved! If she'd have said yes, then I'd never have had the past seven years with you by my side. My regret wasn't that she didn't love me, it was that I was prepared to marry her. No matter what direction I look at it from, it's a good thing that she walked away.'

'It's not a good thing until you can tell me you love me; and mean every word of it. Then I'll believe you that it's a good thing.'

'Jade.'

'Don't Jade me.'

'Jade,' he repeated softly, 'I should have said it years ago, because I certainly felt it. Damn it, I should have said it, and I'm so sorry. I knew you weren't Angela, and I knew everything about you and I was different. Completely different. And I'm sorry that I pulled you back from achieving your dreams. That was wrong. I was just so scared of you disappearing from my life. I told myself that I'd never tell a woman I loved her again unless I meant it.'

As he wiped the tears from Jade's eyes, he wondered how three little words could make so much difference to her life?

Jade placed his hand on her belly. 'Can you feel the baby kicking?'

Shock raced across his face. 'Yes! How long has that been happening?'

'Just now. It's the first time,' she laughed.

Ashley dropped to his knees and held his face alongside her small bump. 'Hello baby.'

They walked back to the penthouse, delirious with their baby's attempts to communicate, and began packing for their trip to India.

Three Little Words

India was stifling. Jade found it far too hot, and stayed in the air-conditioned room. Despite her best intentions, she was going to have to miss the meeting with Serafina after all; and sent her apologies.

The five-star hotel was in the prime business district of Mumbai's Nariman Point. The luxurious setting boasted modern facilities. They'd been in the hotel for two days, enjoying the global cuisine. Ashley had been in the hotel many times before, as it was an ideal location for business meetings when he was in India. The conference rooms on the top floor had sweeping views of the ocean. More than anything, he appreciated the spa and fitness centre being open twenty-four hours a day. It was a godsend when he was struggling with different time zones and body rhythms.

Ashley met Serafina in the hotel restaurant, and within minutes brought her up to their room. There was no way Jade was going to miss this meeting. If there was one thing Ashley learnt the hard way, it was to include Jade in *everything*.

Serafina was deeply empathetic, and said it was important for Jade to put herself first. 'Listen to your body, Jade. Don't push yourself. Pregnancy isn't the time for that.'

Ashley ordered room service, and they discussed the tour and how the flights were for Serafina and her entourage.

'Everything is perfect, just like Jade promised. I know it's early days, but we're talking about another concert in two years from now. How soon would I need to book with you?'

'The sooner the better,' Jade said. 'We know what

your needs are, and if we've got this much notice, it makes both of our jobs easier. What will your next tour be called? Have you written new songs?'

'I've written another twenty songs. None of them have been released. The tour will be called *Just Three Little Words.*'

Jade looked at Ashley, and then back to Serafina. Ashley moved away and poured some more wine.

'Interesting title,' Jade said.

'Yeah, it was based on an old boyfriend who couldn't say "I love you". Needless to say we ended up parting ways.'

'I'm not surprised,' Jade said firmly.

Ashley looked at her, and said 'Actions speak louder than words, Jade.'

Serafina looked at Ashley and asked 'Oh dear, have I just touched a raw nerve?'

'No,' Jade replied, bringing an end to this part of the conversation. 'What are the rest of your songs about?'

They talked deep into the night, and Serafina finally left their suite at 2am.

'I'm so exhausted I feel sick,' Jade complained as she brushed her teeth.

'Let's get you to bed,' Ashley said, reaching for her hand.

'No, I feel *sick.*'

'So come and lie down.'

'Ashley, you're not hearing me. I feel…' and before she could say another word, her entire dinner was over the bathroom floor.

'Jesus, Jade! I'm sorry. I thought you were just a bit queasy.'

Ashley passed her a damp cloth, and said 'I thought the morning sickness was well and truly over?'

'This isn't...' she retched some more. 'This isn't morning sickness.'

Jade sat on the floor, and then lay down against the cool tiles.

'Can you call for the maid to clean this up?' Jade asked.

'I'll do it myself,' he offered.

'But why? Why don't you let someone else do it?'

'Because when you care for someone, you clean up their sick, Jade.'

When everything was in order, he carried her to bed. 'Is there anything I can get you?'

Before Jade could answer, she felt herself gag. 'There can't be any food left in there to bring up. Why is this still happening?'

Ashley held his hand to her brow. 'You've got a temperature. I'm going to call for a doctor.'

'No, don't do that. Please. I'll be okay soon.'

'Jade, I'm not arguing. This isn't just about you. This is also about the baby. *Our* baby.'

Within minutes, a doctor was in their suite examining her.

They deciphered their way through his heavy Indian accent.

'Food poisoning?' Jade asked. 'But we've only eaten from this hotel while we've been here. This is five-star accommodation. We haven't eaten anywhere else.'

'Did you have the cheese salad yesterday?'

'Yes, why?'

'Fifteen other people also have food poisoning tonight. It was the salad. Always the salad that catches people.'

'How long will she be sick, doctor?' Ashley asked.

'A few days maybe. You need to make sure she has plenty of water.'

Jade moved out of the bed, and raced to the toilet and locked the door after her. It was one thing for Ashley to clear up vomit, but diarrhoea was completely off limits. Jade doubled over as the stomach cramps triggered involuntary bowel movements. India was meant to be fun. This was her last exotic jaunt before becoming a mother. Vomiting and diarrhoea were neither exotic nor fun!

'Jade, let me in. I'm concerned about you. I need to look after you.'

'I'm fine.'

There was no way she was going to bed while her body betrayed her in such an undignified way.

'I want to pass some bottled water in to you. Open the door.'

'Later!'

Ashley sat on the floor outside the door.

Jade hated that he spent hours listening to the noises of her evacuating her body. What she didn't know was that he found himself wishing it was him who was sick, and not her.

By five in the morning, he'd had enough. Sleep deprivation was bringing out the worst in him. 'Open this bloody door now or I'll break it down.'

Jade reluctantly opened the door. She stood there, with her eyes sunken into her face, and skin so pale; she looked completely wrung out.

'I'm taking you to a hospital.'

'No. Please don't. I just want to go home. Take me

home.'

Within the hour they were aboard a Lyndhurst plane. Ashley held her hand all the way back to London, insisting that she keep sipping water.

They were met by Ashley's limousine driver, and taken straight to the penthouse.

'If you're not right by the morning,' he said, tucking her up in bed, 'then you're going to hospital, no questions asked.'

'Okay,' she said, crying softly into the pillow.

Ashley held her as the tears flowed. 'I'm sorry it was such an awful experience for you. India can be such fun. If I'd known it was going to end like this, I'd never have taken you.'

'It's not your fault.' Jade sniffed, and snuggled into his arms.

Jade slept soundly for several hours, and was awoken by a sharp pain. Thinking she might be about to heave, she raced to the bathroom. As she squatted by the toilet, a trail of blood trickled on the floor. 'No,' she whispered. 'No, please no.'

Jade lifted her nightie up to reveal legs soaked in blood. As she fell to the floor and sobbed, her cries woke Ashley.

The possibility of miscarriage hadn't even occurred to him. To see the carnage on their bathroom floor was more than either of them could take. They fell into each other's arms, mourning the loss of their baby: the baby who would hold them together through the years ahead. The baby who had come to change their lives.

175

The baby…*the baby who didn't stay.*

'Shall I call a doctor now?'

'No, there's probably no need. My body is expelling everything. It knows what to do. I…' she cried some more. 'I just need to rest. I won't be going into work today.'

'You won't be going into work for the foreseeable future. You'll take all the time you need.'

'And you? When will you go into work?'

'On the same day that you do. And not a moment before.'

As she rocked in his arms, for the first time she realised he was right: *actions do speak louder than words.* If ever she doubted his love for her, she mostly certainly didn't now. Ashley was here for her when she most needed him, and that was all that mattered.

'I'm so sorry, Jade. I know how devastated I feel about this, but it must be so much worse for you since you were the one growing this baby. So much worse.'

For some time he held her close, and then undressed her. 'You get in the shower, and I'll get the mop.'

A few minutes later, he was in the shower with her, washing her hair and soaping her skin. 'I'm so sorry,' he whispered again. 'This should never have happened to you.'

"This happens to women every day, all around the world.'

'That doesn't make it any less traumatic, though, does it?'

His understanding, empathy and compassion soldered something in her heart that day. The warm spray of the shower held them like a healing balm. Later, she sat at the dining table while he changed the

176

bedding. 'Here, have this tea,' he said, bringing over a pot of chamomile. 'Then we'll go back to bed.'

Jade looked Ashley up and down. For more than seven years she'd been by his side for almost every day. Even though he was a tough businessman, he was always kind and courteous. But she'd never seen this side of him before. Ashley Lyndhurst, the man who could pay people to do all the menial jobs, was now capable of mopping up blood, cleaning vomit, and making tea. When did this personality change happen? she wondered. Maybe it was there all along, but she'd just never had a chance to see it. Maybe she'd been too busy cleaning up after him that she never gave him a chance to show his true colours.

Despite her wishes, Ashley called a doctor to examine Jade and assure them that she'd be okay.

'Give it a few months before you try for another baby,' he suggested. 'It's not just the body which needs to heal. Miscarriage is a death, and deserves grieving time.' The doctor touched her lightly on the arm and said 'I'm so sorry for the death of your baby.'

First thing the next morning, Ashley opened the door to Jade's mother.

'Hi Martha. Thanks for coming. Jade could really do with some mothering right now.'

Mrs Stirling wept in his arms. 'She doesn't deserve this. Jade does not deserve this amount of pain.'

'No, she doesn't.' Ashley said, 'She's still sleeping. Can I get you a coffee, tea?'

'Tea would be lovely, thank you.'

Ashley filled a pot, then made them some scrambled eggs for breakfast.

177

Jade slept for the next few hours, and Ashley chatted with his future mother-in-law.

'She never did get over her father leaving. It devastated me, of course, when he left me for his secretary, but Jade was crushed. She had trusted her Dad with her whole heart, and although he never meant to hurt her, she took it personally.'

'Jade's never told me about this before. I knew you divorced when she was young, but she's never shared the reason why. Actually, she rarely talks about her Dad.'

'Jade feels that it's her fault in some way. If she'd been a better daughter, perhaps. If she'd just kept her room tidier. If she got better marks at school. If she looked prettier. For a girl who was always so playful, she became one who tried to become a perfectionist. It nearly drove me nuts, but I could see why she was doing it. She wanted to prove to her father that she was good enough. Jade wanted to be someone he could be proud of. But, as time went on, he removed himself more and more from Jade and her baby brother. It's silly, I know, but she still carries a lot of that childhood pain. She'd really been such a daddy's girl; always sitting on his lap at night having a cuddle. And then, without warning, he wasn't there anymore. He'd see her every other weekend, but only if he had the time.'

'But they still have contact now. Jade phones him from time to time.'

'Yes, but it's more out of obligation than love. Family is important to her. She'd never just cut ties with him, though she threatened to when she heard on the grapevine that he was having another affair.'

Martha started crying. The thought of her daughter miscarrying was too much. Ashley hugged

her and said, 'We'll get through this. I promise. And Martha, I'm not going anywhere. I'm not leaving Jade.'

Martha looked up at him through her wet, red eyes. 'She's been in love with you for so long. It would break my heart, too, if you walked away.'

'Well we can't have that, can we?' he chuckled softly. 'Two broken hearts would really ruin my reputation.' Ashley's smile eased her pain, and she reached for his hand. 'You're a good man, Ashley. I can see why she's fallen so hard for you.'

Jade and Martha spent the next two weeks snuggled on the sofa, sipping tea, reading books, chatting, crying, laughing, watching daytime TV, and eating chocolate brownies. Ashley continued to work from home, and from time to time he looked across at his fiancée and her mother and wondered if Jade's visitations to the Underworld were more about her father than about him. Perhaps the alfalfa situation was to do with years of built-up and unexpressed anger towards her father's affair? It made sense. No matter how often he'd thought about Jade's actions, he'd never been able to reconcile the level of destruction with *his* actions. It was time to put to rest ghosts left by George Stirling. Jade needed to know, in no uncertain terms, that she couldn't spend the rest of her life making Ashley pay for the sins of her father.

When Martha left to go back to Devon, Jade knew it was time to get on with life. With a heavy heart, she made plans to start work again at the office.

A fortnight after her miscarriage, Jade said they could both do with getting some fresh air. Ashley kissed her on the forehead, and asked 'What do you have in mind?'

'Perhaps a little walk by the river?'

'Of course. Let's get you rugged up well, though,' he said. It made her smile that he was being so protective, but she knew he couldn't keep her wrapped in cotton wool forever. The truth was that life sometimes dealt cruel blows. There was a time for licking your wounds, and a time for stepping out into the world wearing the pain in your heart forever.

She was soon wrapped in a thick coat. Ashley was wearing his favourite ivory-coloured jumper, and faded denims.

They walked for about fifteen minutes, and then stopped beneath a red oak tree. The leaves were vibrant, and the air was chilly.

Ashley brought Jade to face him. Despite the trauma of the past couple of weeks, he was surprised to see how well she looked. Maybe it was the Autumn air? Ashley studied her face, as he'd done so many times before: the almond-shaped eyes, defined cheekbones, dimples; and inviting red, rosebud lips; and the way her chocolate-coloured hair, hung down in waves, and matched the hue of her eyes perfectly.

'Ashley, I want to have children with you. I want ten bouncing babies with you, but…but not yet. Let's wait. I feel like I've waited so long for you, and now that you're here…Now that you're *really* in my life, I just want to enjoy you. I want to enjoy us, without nappies and colic and teething. There is plenty of time for all of that, and when it happens I'll really embrace it, but for now, I just want you. All of you, and nothing less. Please let me have that.' Jade looked at him there, all handsome in his jumper and jeans, desperately wishing he was naked so she could get a bit closer to him.

'And I want all of you,' he whispered, holding her as closely as possible. Ashley kissed her softly, then hungrily. Perhaps that comfortable cable jumper was going to end up on the Autumn leaves after all. He fought against every primal urge in his body, and extricated himself from her lips. His fingers brushed slightly against her cheek.

'Jade, I can't live without you. I don't want to live without you. You're my whole world.' For a moment, he stopped talking so that he could kiss her.

'I love you, my darling. I truly love you.'

Jade blinked. Had Ashley actually, *finally*, just said that he loved her? Impossible! She must have imagined it. Those three words, in that order? Not, "you're loveable", but *I love you*? That kiss must have made her wish that he'd said it to her.

'These aren't just words,' he continued. 'Even if I say it ten times a day for the rest of our lives, it will mean the same thing every single time: you are my world. You are my life. You are my everything. I love you, Jade Stirling. I always have.'

'I know you love me,' she cried with joy. 'I've always known it, but oh my goodness, I can't tell you what it means to me to finally hear you say it. Tell me again!' she laughed, as he held her tight.

'I love you, Jade. I love you, I love you, I love you.'
'And again?'
'I love you!'

On The Wings of Dreams

The wedding was postponed, and postponed, and postponed. Jade insisted that the wedding would happen when the time was right. Ashley didn't argue. He'd come to appreciate Jade's determined, and stubborn, attitude about many things in their lives. There were times for letting her have her way, and times for putting his foot down. The wedding date was not something to argue over.

The right time just happened to be the following Summer. There'd been a lot of changes in their lives, and with each new one, they took their time adjusting to them.

Lyndhurst Incorporated grew substantially as a result of the Serafina Simmo tour, and Ashley decided it was time to advertise the new role.

It wasn't a PA he was trying to find, but someone to fill his shoes. The priority for him was providing a solid foundation to family life, and he wanted to take more of a back seat in his company. He'd still oversee operations, but employed a new chief executive, and two managers.

Jade began publishing the in-air magazine, and spent much of her time working from home. She employed two PAs for the new chief executive, and didn't relinquish her position until she felt fully satisfied that they could do her job properly.

A baby girl arrived in their lives the following year in early June. Skye Summer Lyndhurst was bonny, and healthy, and had her mother's chocolate-coloured, almond-shaped eyes and dark hair; and her father's smile. As she sat upon Ashley's hip that beautiful Summer's day in late August, they walked around the perimeter of his sisters' organic farm. The girls had done a great job keeping it going, and he knew his Mum would be pleased. Skye's aunties fussed around her all morning, barely letting the baby back in her parents' arms.

'We want Skye to know her aunties, and that means you're going to be seeing a lot more of us,' Ashley said. 'That's why we've just bought the property next door.'

Ashley's sisters looked at each other. 'Why? What for?'

'We don't want to be under your feet, but we want Skye to spend as much time running around the fields and climbing trees as possible. The end of that farm is five miles from here. It's pretty substantial, as you know. We're going to put in a small flying school for teenagers, and the farm has a cottage as well as the farmhouse. Jade's mum is going to be moving up here so she can have a hands-on role with her granddaughter.'

'Where's my brother, and what you have you done with him?' Kat laughed. 'What happened to the businessman of the year?'

'I'm a father now. Family is everything.'

Ashley squeezed Jade's hand. 'It's everything.'

Jade smiled at him, and squeezed his hand back. 'Well, we're going to need all that space when the twins arrive.'

Ashley's face went white. 'Twins? *Twins?*'

Jade and Ashley's sisters all laughed out loud. They laughed so hard they started crying.

'We're having twins?' Ashley asked as he looked at Skye bouncing on his hip and pulling at his stubble. They were going to have two more children? 'I know I'm a twin and it increases our chances of having twins, but *two* children?'

'Just kidding!' Jade laughed.

~ The End ~

184

Novels by Veronika Robinson

Mosaic
Bluey's Cafe

The Gypsy Moon Trilogy
Sisters of the Silver Moon
Behind Closed Doors
Flowers in Her Hair

Sweet Cinnamon Romance
Love at the Treble Clef Cafe
Love in a Scottish Storm
On the Wings of Love
Recipe for Love
House of Hearts

Moonlight and Motif
(magical realism novels publishing in 2023)
The Button Tin
The Soapmaker
The Irish Dollmaker

For a list of the author's non-fiction titles, visit
www.veronikarobinson.com

About The Artist: *Heidi Harbers*

Happiest when she's brightening up the world, whether it's decorating a room, painting a mural, growing a garden, feeding her chickens avocados, or organising fun events in her village, creativity is at the heart of Heidi's life.

As a pub landlady, and former restaurant owner, she has cooked for thousands of people across the years, serving up delicious meals, both traditional and unusual. When not cooking, Heidi's flare for transforming bare walls into canvases for her community to enjoy has earned her a wonderful reputation.

Australian born and raised, Heidi has travelled the world; and for many years has called England home. Born under the zodiac sign of Libra, the lovers, it is only natural that her art has found a home on the covers of romance novels.

Review This Book

As an indie author, it would mean the world to me if you would be so kind as to leave a review of this book online.

I wish you the BEST day ever!

Veronika x